MW00803598

WATER GHOST

WATER GHOST

by Ching Yeung Russell

illustrated by Christopher Zhong-Yuan Zhang

BOYDS MILLS PRESS

Special thanks to my editor, Karen Klockner, for believing in my work, and to my husband, Phillip Russell, for his tremendous help — C.Y.R.

Text copyright © 1995 by Christina Ching Yeung Russell
Illustrations copyright © 1995 by Boyds Mills Press

Published by Caroline House
Boyds Mills Press, Inc.
A Highlights Company
815 Church Street
Honesdale, Pennsylvania 18431
Printed in the United States of America

Publisher Cataloging-in-Publication Data
Russell, Ching Yeung.
Water ghost / by Ching Yeung Russell ; illustrated by
Christopher Zhong-Yuan Zhang.—1st ed.
[192]p. : ill. ;   cm.
Summary : Living in China during the late 1940s, Ying gives all her
hard-earned money to the grandmother of a classmate who has drowned.
ISBN 1-56397-413-4
1. China—Social conditions—1912-1949—Juvenile fiction.
2. Death—Fiction—Juvenile literature.
[1. China—Social conditions—1912-1949—Fiction. 2. Death—Fiction.]
I. Zhang, Christopher Zhong-Yuan, ill. II. Title.
[F]—dc20   1995
Library of Congress Catalog Card Number 94-74534

First edition, 1995
Book designed by Jean Krulis
The text of this book is set in 14-point Galliard.
Distributed by St. Martin's Press

10 9 8 7 6 5 4 3 2 1

To my uncles who helped raise me and
never asked anything in return,

and

To all my childhood friends
I left behind

— C.Y.R.

CHAPTER 1

*T*he whole fourth-grade class went wild when Mrs. Yu, our homeroom and literature teacher, announced that the school would hold its second annual schoolwide camp-out on Children's Day, April 4. Students in the fourth grade and up would be eligible to go. I had waited a long time for this day.

Last year my twelve-year-old cousin, Kee, went. I couldn't go because I was only in the third grade. He had bragged for the rest of the year about what he had done. I really envied him.

Do you know what they did? First they had a cooking contest, then they made a bonfire. They sang and played around until midnight. When they went to sleep, each one had to take a turn guarding the tents like soldiers in a war. They had made an agreement with the students from Good-Luck Primary School, who were going to disguise themselves as our enemy. The "enemy" would sneak up at night and try to "steal" our cooking equipment. So the students from our school had to be on guard all night.

I could hardly wait for school to be out. Without waiting for Ah Mei, my best friend, to walk home with me, I ran all the way to tell Ah Pau the good news.

But Ah Pau was not home.

"Where is Ah Pau?" I asked Ah So, Kee's seventeen-year-old sister, who was embroidering in the living room. "Has she gone to the market?"

"I'm not sure," Ah So said without raising her head.

Kee breezed in. He was very excited.

I asked, "Do you plan to go to the camp-out?"

"Anyone who doesn't plan to go is stupid! Are you going?"

"Of course!"

"Do you think Grandma will let you go?"

"Why not?"

"A lot of reasons."

I suddenly felt as if somebody had hit me in the head. I knew I would have to work hard to persuade Ah Pau to give me permission to go. She was the one who had taken care of me since I was five, when I came to live with her family in Chan Village. Our village was in the town of Tai Kong, about seventy-five miles southeast of Canton. My parents were in Hong Kong.

"What will I do if Ah Pau will not let me go?" I asked.

"You need to find the right time to convince her, step by step."

"How?"

"How? Use your brain, knucklehead!"

"Please tell me how I can convince her to let me go. Will you, pleeease?"

"What's in it for me?"

"Tomorrow I will give you my snack."

"Don't forget. Otherwise, you'll regret it."

"I won't. Tell me now."

"Well, the best way is to try to please her and make her feel that you are a good girl."

"How?"

"Stupid! For example, do your homework first, so she won't be upset about it not being done."

"Then what? Oh, I know!" I hurriedly went upstairs to do my homework instead of goofing off with a whole bunch of cousins at the Chan Village plaza. I didn't have much homework; we had just finished midterm exams the week before.

I heard footsteps. I recognized them as Ah Pau's. "A lot of homework?" she asked.

"No." I almost wanted to tell her about the camp-out. I was glad I didn't. She probably

would say she had a lot on her mind. I asked,
"Have you gone to the market yet? I want to
go with you."

"I am ready to go now. Have you finished
your homework yet?"

"Yes. Am I a good girl? I did my homework
before you even told me to."

"Yes, you are," Ah Pau said.

I hurriedly put my homework back into my
wicker bookbag and walked in front of her so she
wouldn't trip on the stairs. She was seventy-one
years old.

"I'll help you hold the basket, too, Ah
Pau!" I took the long-handled basket from the
kitchen wall and carried it on my shoulder.

CHAPTER 2

*T*he market was at the south side of the town, at the end of Tai Gai, the main street. It was about four o'clock in the afternoon. The October sun had slanted over the street, leaving one side of the street bathed in sunshine. It was noisy and crowded. Vendors called out to customers for their attention.

"Fresh *bok choi*! Only five cents a catty!"

"Big fat seasonal snails! Look at them before you buy!"

"Fat pork for the best pork oil!"

But their calling didn't stop the grandmas and their grandchildren from strolling by each stall. They checked vegetables, meat, and fish sold on both sides of the street for a good bargain.

Ah Pau and I strolled by the fish stall. The vendor called, "Ma'am, look at these lively croakers!"

Ah Pau stopped.

"Are you going to buy fish, Ah Pau?"

There was a water irrigation system made out of bamboo pipe. Water shot out from the bamboo pipe and down to the shallow, round wooden tub. Several croakers were swimming inside the container.

"What is the price for the croakers?" Ah Pau asked the vendor.

"One *yuan* a catty," the man said.

The dark gray fish swam around slowly in the shallow water.

"The price is up," Ah Pau mumbled. "How about eighty cents for a catty?" Ah Pau asked, pretending she was about to leave.

The man thought for a second. He said, "Okay," before she went off somewhere else. The man motioned Ah Pau back. "Just this time."

"Let me choose one for you, Ah Pau," I said enthusiastically. I had studied which one was the biggest while Ah Pau was bargaining with the man. "Get that one, Ah Pau! It's the biggest."

"All right," the man said, scooping up the fish with a small net. Then he caught the fish's gill with his scale hook. The fish curled up in the air and wriggled around.

"Is your scale accurate?" Ah Pau asked the man.

"Of course," the man said. "Exactly one and a half catties—one *yuan* and twenty cents ma'am."

"Whew, too much," Ah Pau mumbled. "Get a smaller one."

The man put the fish back into the water. A little string of blood floated into the water around its gill.

"Why don't we get that one, Ah Pau?"

"Too expensive."

"How about this one?" I pointed to another one.

"Is this about a catty?" Ah Pau asked.

"It looks like it," the vendor said. He scooped up the fish and weighed it. "About one catty. It would be eighty cents. Is it okay?"

Ah Pau asked, "Forty cents less than the other one?"

The man said, "Yes."

After Ah Pau gave the money to the man, the man started to clean the fish.

"Save the gills for our cat," Ah Pau reminded him.

"All right."

"And make sure not to break the gallbladder. I want to eat the intestines," I added. Kee and I always took turns eating the fish guts.

The man carefully slit the stomach of the

fish. He slowly pulled the guts outside. Boy! I was lucky! The guts appeared to be pinkish instead of a muddy color. That meant the intestines were edible. He pulled out the gallbladder from among the guts. Then he put the guts back, wrapped the fish and gills with a banana leaf, tied it with a string of dried sea grass, and handed it to me.

"Thank you," the man said.

Blood dripped from the banana leaf as I dropped it into the basket. We left and wandered around other stalls.

As Ah Pau and I walked, I heard someone yell, "Get out of here, cripple!"

I looked toward the place where the sound came from. It was someone yelling at Cripple Yip. She was trying to pick up discarded yellow *bok choi* leaves in front of a *bok choi* stall.

"You see the crippled girl, Ah Pau?" I whispered to her. "She's new—from another town. She sits behind me at school, all by herself."

"Oh," Ah Pau said, looking at Cripple Yip,

who hobbled away with an old lady.

"Who is that old lady with her?"

"It's her grandma. The girl lives with her now."

Then Ah Pau bought a bunch of lettuce. She also asked for a couple of green onions, which the vegetable vendors often gave away.

"That's all, Ah Pau?"

"Yes, we have dried turnip at home."

So I carried the basket on my shoulder, and we headed for home.

"Mercy! Mercy!" An old beggar was kneeling not far from the market. She bowed her head on the ground and said "Mercy!" to whomever walked by.

I was anxious to get back, waiting for the best chance to tell Ah Pau the good news. But Ah Pau stopped and dropped forty cents into the beggar's clay dish.

At first, I was stunned. Forty cents was a lot of money. Four more forty cents could be enough for my camp-out! I hadn't seen Ah Pau be that generous before. Most of the time she just offered one cent. Never before had I seen her give away that much money.

I wanted to ask her why, but I didn't want her to be upset over my question. In fact, I was glad she was so generous. That meant she had money for my camp-out!

CHAPTER 3

I gave the basket to Ah So. She was learning from Auntie how to cook so that when she got married, her husband's parents wouldn't blame Auntie and Ah Pau for not teaching her how to be a traditional housewife. I hurriedly got Ah Pau's silver water pipe. I lit up a long, skinny paper stick and gave it to Ah Pau. I knew that when Ah Pau smoked her water pipe, it was a time when she did not have a lot on her mind.

"Ah Pau, I have already gotten your water pipe." I tried to be as calm as I could. I moved the stool that Kee had made for her seventy-first birthday to the right position so she could lean on the door. I said, "Ah Pau, sit."

"You are working awfully hard. What is on your mind?" Ah Pau asked.

"Oh. . . ." I was embarrassed that Ah Pau saw through me so easily, but I knew it was the right moment to ask her. I sat on the clay floor next to her and said, "See, Uncle always says that reading ten thousand books is not as beneficial as traveling one thousand miles. That means you will get more education from going out to see the world than just studying inside."

"So, what are you up to?" Ah Pau got a little tobacco from the tobacco container in the pipe and lit it.

"I want to get more education, so I want to go to the camp-out next spring." I was sure

that Ah Pau wouldn't care about the fun, just the education.

"They're holding that again?"

"Yes. Because the teachers said it's good for the students. That's why they will have it a second time. I have never been camping before. I have been waiting for a whole year!"

Ah Pau continued to smoke. The water in the water pipe made a *boh boh boh* noise. Then she blew the ashes on the floor and started fresh tobacco. It made me more nervous.

"See, Ah Pau, I'm a good girl. I have already finished all my homework. I helped you carry the basket and helped you choose the fish. I helped you get your water pipe and lit the paper stick for you. Can you reward me by letting me go to the camp-out?"

Ah Pau laughed and teased me, "Oh, you did all that just for a reward, huh?"

"Please, Ah Pau." I knew Ah Pau would say that I was too young and couldn't take care of myself. She didn't even let me go to the school picnic. She was afraid that I would get hurt.

She would feel guilty if something bad happened to me and there was no way to inform my parents, since we didn't have a way to contact each other. "Please, Ah Pau. I have never even gone to a picnic. I am a big girl. I'm already ten. Please, Ah Pau."

Without waiting for Ah Pau to answer me, I added, "Besides that, Kee is going, too. He can keep an eye on me."

"I can't really trust Kee. When he's out playing, he forgets everything, even his own last name."

"But there are teachers, and all my schoolmates are older than I am. They can keep an eye on me."

Ah Pau didn't answer me. She just smoked. Then she said, "Is Ah Mei going, too?"

Oh, no. Ah Pau admired Ah Mei because she was always the number one student in the class. I was only average. I suddenly felt very discouraged. If Ah Mei were going, I would have a better chance. I mumbled, "Ah Mei doesn't like camping. She doesn't like that kind of stuff."

"I don't think it is a good idea to spend a night on the hill."

"How come Kee can go and I can't?"

"Kee is a boy, and you are a girl."

"What's the difference? Except he stands up to pee and I squat down!"

Ah Pau burst into laughter. "It's not just about squatting down or standing up."

"But it's unfair. Kee can go and I can't."

"Your auntie let Kee go, not me."

"May I ask Auntie if she would let me go?"

"I don't think Auntie can make a decision about that."

She was right, because I was not Auntie's daughter.

"Besides that, the hill is so dirty. I don't understand why your teachers plan that kind of outing."

I knew what Ah Pau meant by "dirty." She meant there were ghosts and spirits there. So I said, "I go to Buddhist Hill to collect pine straw. So what is the difference?"

"You go in the daytime, not to spend the night."

"I can carry a red handkerchief all the time. And also, my hair strings are red."

Ah Pau didn't say a word. I added, "I can even take a weeping willow stick with me, okay?"

Ah Pau always told me that wearing red and carrying a weeping willow stick were the best ways to get rid of ghosts. That's why Ah Pau never let me wear blue or white on my head, especially white. White meant death.

"How will you go to the bathroom?"

"I will remember to chant before I pee, 'Please forgive me for peeing, because I'm an innocent girl and I can't tell right from wrong.'"

Ah Pau often instructed me to chant those words whenever I needed to go to the bath-room on the hillside. It was in case I acciden-tally peed on a dead person buried there. To do that would irritate the dead person, and his skull would roll and roll after me until I turned a ninety-degree corner. "I always say that, Ah Pau."

"How much is the fee?"

"So you'll let me go?" I almost jumped to the ceiling. "You are the best Ah Pau I have ever had!"

"Don't be so excited," Ah Pau laughed. Her gold-and-jade earrings from her seventy-first birthday made a tinkling sound.

"It is only two *yuan*."

"Two *yuan*! That's more than two meals cost!" Ah Pau cried.

"But you gave forty cents to that old beggar today!"

"That's different. I just pitied her. She doesn't have any family."

"We are not rich."

"I know. But we have each other. You are still young, and you don't understand. It's very, very pitiful when you are poor and old and sick and there's nobody to take care of you. So, we just eat a little less, but it might help her a great deal."

"When I am grown-up and rich I will give money to the poor, too. So would you please let me go?"

"That's an awful lot of money for just a couple of days."

"I know." I knew Ah Pau was wavering, so I jumped on the chance before she could change her mind. "If I pay the fee myself, can I go? Please, Ah Pau! I have been waiting for a whole year!"

"Well, I don't know how you can get that much money."

I knew I had a chance now, so I quickly bargained. "If I can find that much money, can I go?"

"Well, I guess so."

"Oh, thanks, Ah Pau! You are the best Ah Pau in the whole wide world!" I hugged her and almost knocked her off the stool. Before she could change her mind, I sealed the bargain by hooking her little finger and mine three times. I pulled out one hair and threw it in the air and spit on the floor. Then I declared, "Ah Pau, if you change your mind, you have to find my hair and lick my spit!"

Ah Pau laughed and said, "I still don't know how you can save that much money."

"I can save all my *lai see* money that I get at Chinese New Year. That's why the school announced the camp-out ahead of time."

"Wait a minute! Don't forget that you and I had a deal," Kee butted in from behind.

"What deal?"

"Don't act like a dummy! You promised to pay me all your *lai see* money for borrowing my junk to buy an apple last fall, remember?"

"Oh . . . yeah. Could I . . . maybe postpone paying you until next year?"

"Are you kidding? Do you think I'm a charity organization or something? I've already let you postpone paying it for one year."

"But that didn't count. Remember how we gave all our *lai see* money to Ah Pau's sister so she could see the doctor last year?"

Kee was quiet, so I begged, "Please . . ."

"No!"

"I can give you my snacks from now on."

"No!"

"Who cares? I can look for more junk to sell."

"Go ahead. Everybody would be rich if they could make two *yuan* in just a few months collecting junk."

That was true—it would take a long time to make that much money collecting broken glass, scrap metal, or duck feathers to sell to the junk man.

"Well, you just try your best, and I'll see if I can help you make up the rest," Ah Pau stated. She was always on my side.

"That's unfair, Grandma!" Kee protested. "Last year I had to pay the fee myself. If you make up hers, you have to make up mine, too."

"Well, I'll leave you both alone. I don't intend to play favorites. You both will have to pay your own fee if you want to go camping."

Kee gave me a triumphant grin.

"Shut up!" I told him, and gave him a hard look.

CHAPTER 4

When we were ready for supper, I helped take the dishes to the dining table. I put the fish head toward Kee's seat. It was his turn to eat the fish head—our favorite treat that we always fought for. Later I changed it toward my seat, hoping that Kee would forget it was his turn. After we sat down, I said, "Kee, if I let you have the fish head and the intestines, could I pay the money back to you after next New Year?"

"Trying to cheat me, huh? It's *my* turn, remember?" He turned the fish head back.

Boy! I couldn't fool him. I poured lettuce broth into the hot rice and put in some salty dried turnips, waiting for the fish bone. For Kee and me, the head and intestines were the best, then the bone, then the meat.

Auntie used a different pair of chopsticks to pick up the food from the plates because of her cough. She dipped the cooked lettuce lightly into the soy sauce and suggested, "Why don't you let Ah So teach you how to embroider?"

"*Her?*" Kee laughed loudly. "Her fingers are as big as bananas!"

"Kee!" Auntie stopped him. "It's not nice to always pour cold water on your cousin."

"But it's true!" Kee did not mind his mother as he did his father. His father ate dinner at his small dry-foods grocery store every night. "I have never seen her hold a needle in all my

life." Then he put the whole set of intestines into his mouth.

"I don't mind teaching her as long as she can sit still for a couple of hours each day," Ah So said. She gracefully put rice into her mouth, then closed her mouth to chew.

"I sure wish she could learn. She has to learn some girl things—better than always running around like a boy," Ah Pau commented.

"It's so boring to sit and sit," I protested.

"At least you have to learn how to hold the needle," Ah Pau said, "so later on you can mend your own clothes."

"I don't need to mend them myself. I'll be very rich and have a servant to do that stuff."

"I hope you will be, Ying," Auntie said.

"Yeeh! Dummy! If you can afford a servant, do you think you will still wear clothes that need to be mended, huh?" Kee chided.

"I can wear whatever I want," I said.

"Don't start during the meal!" Ah Pau warned before Kee could fight back.

About a week later at suppertime, Ah Pau

suddenly stopped eating. Her face showed she was in pain.

"What's wrong, Ah Pau?"

"I will be okay. I just ate a little too fast," Ah Pau said. "The food couldn't completely go down to my stomach."

But Ah Pau was not okay. It hurt so much that she had to put the bowl on top of her head and use the chopsticks to tap inside the bottom of the bowl. She hoped the food would go down. But it didn't help this time; I could tell from her expression.

"Are you still hurting very bad, Ah Pau?" I was about to cry. Every time Ah Pau had pain that I couldn't help, I wished I had the pain instead of my Ah Pau.

"Lie down and see if it will help," Auntie suggested.

I helped Ah Pau back to the room that she and I shared.

"How do you feel now, Ah Pau?" I stood at her bedside, as she did when I was sick.

"Better."

"I am glad, Ah Pau. I wished I had the pain, not you. But my wish did not come true." My eyes were wet again, but I didn't want Ah Pau to see my eyes. I didn't want her to be upset over me.

Ah Pau said, "You are such a sweet girl. I feel much better now. You go back to finish your rice."

"I have already finished. I'll go call the ducks back so you can rest more. Okay?"

"Okay. Take the duck dish with you. I'm not sure whether they will mind you as they mind me," Ah Pau said, because she was the one who always took care of the ducks.

I took the duck dish and the chicken fence with me. The chicken fence was woven with bamboo strips. It was about three feet tall and ten feet long. People enclosed both ends to make a circle so the ducks or chickens would not wander away.

CHAPTER 5

*T*he pond was huge. It was at the end of Chan Village at the foot of Ford Hill, next to the waste land. There was a big granite rock extending from Ford Hill; we used the rock as the shore. The rest of the pond was surrounded by trees. At the other side of the pond were houses belonging to other people. By the time I arrived, Ah Mei was there. She had just finished washing out their chamber pot and was ready to leave. "I'll wait for you," she said.

"Okay. *Whaah*—look at the sunset! Isn't it beautiful?" I said. The big orange sun was at the edge of the colorful sky far away. Thousands of fish-scale waves glittered under the setting sun. Several groups of ducks swam leisurely on the pond. The clouds, the sunset, the trees, and the ducks were all reflected in the water. "It looks like a beautiful painting."

"It does," Ah Mei said.

I blocked the sun rays with my hand and found our brown and gray ducks not far away from the shore. I raised up their dish and called out from the bottom of my lungs, "*Gaaa-ga-ga-ga-gaaa! Gaaa-ga-ga-ga-gaaa!*"

About five minutes later, they began to swim toward us. Ah Pau was right; the dish could trick them to come. When they were about five feet away from us, the one in the lead hesitated, then let out a sharp cry, "*Whack! Whack!*" to warn the others. At once, they scattered around in panic and ran and flew with their wings flapping in the air.

"What happened? Why did they do that?" I asked.

"I don't know," Ah Mei said. She started looking at the water and then cried, "Water snake!"

"Where?"

"It's coming toward you!"

I jumped back. "Where?"

"See?"

I looked carefully where Ah Mei was pointing, then said, "Oh, it looks like a big *sahng yu*, not a snake."

"Really?" Ah Mei came closer to look.

"See? Hey! Something bit its head. See the bloody stream around its head?"

"Oh, yes. I wonder what bit him," Ah Mei said.

Sahng yu were very, very expensive. Most of the time, they were cooked with watercress for soup. The soup and meat were good for persons who had had an operation, to make them heal fast and build up their blood.

"I am going to get it for Ah Pau to eat," I said, because the fish was still swimming slowly toward the shore.

"You are not afraid?" Ah Mei asked me. She sounded scared.

"Oh—" I hesitated. We knew that we were not supposed to pick up anything, like a flower or even your own hat, that was blown into the water.

"They are lures for the water ghosts—" I could almost hear Ah Pau reminding me. "The water ghost uses things to attract little children. When the children wade into the water to pick up a flower or whatever, the water ghost makes the flower or your hat float farther and farther away from the shore. The children follow it and try to get it. The water ghost will pull the children down and drown them. So, no matter what it is, *don't* try to pick it up. I'll buy it for you no matter how expensive it is!"

But I couldn't help it, because the fish was coming closer and closer to me. I would be

able to pick it up without wading into the water. "I am going to get it," I said.

"You'd better not," Ah Mei warned me again.

"I'll be careful. I won't go in the water."

So I put down the dish, held the chicken fence with both hands, and reached out quickly. I trapped the fish inside the fence. But the fish didn't try to escape or even struggle. I quickly dragged the fence with the fish onto shore. It still didn't struggle, and looked almost dead, with only its mouth moving up and down gulping for air.

"It's about to die," Ah Mei said. She wasn't as scared as when I was trying to get the fish.

"I know. But it's beautiful," I said. It had a dark gray back, and black spots were all over its body except for its white stomach.

"It's huge, too. I bet it's two feet long!" Ah Mei said.

"I think so. See its body? It is even bigger than my upper arm."

"Bigger than mine, too," Ah Mei said.

I bent over to pick up the fish. Boy, it was so slimy and heavy that I couldn't hold it with just one hand.

"Why don't you hold it with both hands," Ah Mei suggested. "I'll help you take the chicken fence back home."

Afraid the fish would suddenly jump back into the water, I held it tightly up to my chest, as if I were holding a baby, and ran back home.

Ah Mei was as excited as I was. As soon as we stepped into the plaza, she announced loudly, "A big *sahng yu*! Ying caught a giant *sahng yu*!"

All my cousins who were playing or eating their supper at the plaza cried out loudly, "*Whaah!* A giant fish! Come see the giant fish!" They followed me inside my house, all yelling at once.

"Ah Pau! Ah Pau! A giant *sahng yu* for you!" I called out as I stepped in. Ah Pau was feeling better now. She was putting sawdust in the corner of the courtyard for the ducks.

Her mouth fell wide open when she saw the *sahng yu*. "How did you get such a big fish?"

"Yes, how did you get it?" Auntie and Ah So came out.

"I used the chicken fence. It swam toward me. It didn't struggle at all. Its head is injured. It's heavy. Ah Pau, I'm about to drop it!"

"Here! Here!" Ah Pau hurriedly put down the bag of sawdust and placed our wash pan on the ground. "Put it into the pan before you drop it!"

So I carefully laid it in the wash pan, but the fish was so long that about half of its body stuck out.

Ah Pau gently poured some water into the pan. She said, "You can go to the camp for sure, Ying."

"What?"

"I can sell the fish for even more than your camp fee."

"Really? But I caught it for you! I want you to have more blood!"

"Thank you for always thinking about me,

Ying. But you need the camp fee. Early tomorrow morning I will take it to the restaurant and sell it."

"Oh, thanks, Ah Pau! Next time I catch another one, I'll really give it to you. Okay?"

Ah Pau just smiled and said, "I don't think you'll have that kind of luck again so easily."

By now our courtyard was full of my cousins, all squatting down around the pan to look. Some of them popped the fish with their fingers. Suddenly I heard Kee's voice. "Don't touch the fish. You will bother him!"

He was as excited as I was. I knew it because I heard him say, "I bet it would cost at least ten *yuan*!"

"No, more than that! It's worth at least twenty *yuan*!" Ah Man said. He was Ah Mei's brother, the same age as Kee.

I was so happy that I could find the camp fee as easily as snapping my fingers! If I could go back to that same spot and catch a fish every day, I could be a millionaire pretty soon.

I wouldn't need to beg from Kee, and he couldn't cheat me anymore.

Other grandmas and aunties from the village also came to see my fish. When someone came, I had to describe my adventure again. My mouth was dry, but I felt like a real heroine.

"I have never seen such a big *sahng yu* before," Ah Mei's grandma, who was about the same age as Ah Pau, mumbled out loud. Then she raised her face and frowned. "Have you?"

"I haven't, either," Ah Pau said. She seemed to worry about something suddenly, and her happy mood changed. Then she asked me, "Did you say it swam toward you?"

"Yes. After I saw our ducks suddenly swim away. They looked scared. Then I saw the *sahng yu*."

"But it didn't struggle all the time?"

"No. It was almost dead. Its head is injured. Something must have bitten it, Ah Pau."

"It's strange, don't you think so?" Ah Mei's

grandma said to Ah Pau. I saw Ah Pau's mouth drop.

Ah Mei's grandma nodded her head and added, "All the *sahng yu* are no more than a foot long, and they are always very strong and hard to clean. That's where the name *sahng yu* comes from."

"That's what I thought," Ah Pau said. She was very worried.

"You don't like my *sahng yu*, Ah Pau?" I knew something was really bothering her.

But she didn't answer me. She looked as if a lot was on her mind.

CHAPTER 6

*E*verybody in my class knew that I caught a giant *sahng yu*. Everybody was envious that I could get the camp fee so easily, even that bully, Ng Shing, who shared a desk with me. He kept saying, "So what!" I could tell that he was jealous.

Almost everyone, except Cripple Yip, asked me how I caught it. Then I had to tell them again and again. Even though Cripple Yip didn't join in our conversation, I could tell that she was listening—she hadn't turned the page on the book she was reading the whole time we were talking.

"Someday I'd like to go home with you, and you can show me the spot," Ming Ming said.

"Stupid! Do you think she would show it to you?" Ng Shing said.

"Why not? I can show her."

"I'd like to go, too," Ping Ping said. "From now on, I'll start paying more attention to the water when I walk around the pond."

"Me, too," Ming Ming said.

"Maybe you can catch a fish even bigger than mine," I joked.

"I hope so," Ping Ping laughed.

We all laughed.

"Ah Pau! Have you sold my *sahng yu* yet?" I called out loudly before I even put down my bookbag.

Ah Pau came out from the kitchen to meet me. She really looked as if she had a lot on her mind. "I have something to tell you," she said.

"What's that, Ah Pau? Are you not feeling well?"

"No. I am all right. I want to tell you that I'm sorry. I had to let the fish go."

"What?"

"I let the fish go back to the pond last night. I didn't want to upset you before you went to school."

"Why?" I couldn't believe what she said. "I already told my friends that I had the camp fee."

"Why, Grandma?" I heard Kee ask from behind.

Ah Pau didn't answer us. Instead she asked, "Do you know what we do before we cook the *sahng yu*?"

"Yes," I said. "Auntie always throws it very hard on the ground several times until it is about half dead, then she starts to clean it. Auntie said it's the only way to hold it down to clean it."

"But the fish didn't even struggle at all," Ah Pau pointed out.

"That's because it was injured, Ah Pau."

"Do you know why it was injured?"

"Something bit it."

"Why did something bite it? It's only a trick."

"You mean the water ghost's trick?" Suddenly I felt a chill.

"Yes. This is the third year," Ah Pau said.

"What do you mean?"

"Every three years someone drowns. That means the ghost wants someone to take its place every three years. Do you remember a girl drowned exactly three years ago?"

"Yes—at the dam around our school," Kee said. But I didn't remember it.

"This is the third year." Ah Pau's face looked scared.

Kee mumbled, "But it was at the dam around school, not this pond."

"They can move. It is just like people moving from one place to another."

"I'm scared, Ah Pau."

"You don't need to be scared," Ah Pau said as she hugged me. "Last night when I let the fish go, I also thanked Buddha for looking after you."

"What should I do now?"

"Just stay away from the water. Ah Mei's grandma said that the water ghosts will not give up. They'll try another way to attract their victims."

"I'll listen to you, Ah Pau."

"Me, too, Grandma," said Kee.

"Good boy. Good girl. I hope you are not mad at me for letting the fish go before telling you, Ying. I didn't want to wait until morning; the fish might not have lived."

"I am not mad at you. I have never been mad at you, Ah Pau."

"That's good."

"Well . . ." Kee was very sympathetic this time. He said, "It looks as if you'll have to wait another year to go to the camp-out."

I should have grabbed that chance and

asked him to let me postpone paying back the *lai see* money, but I wasn't able to think of anything at that moment.

Ah Pau said, "No, Kee." Her face lit up. "I think she will be able to make the money soon."

"How?"

"I'm not sure yet, but my right eyelid jumped several times right after I let the *sahng yu* go."

"I hope you're right, Ah Pau," I said. She often told me that if the left eyelid jumped, it meant bad luck; but if the right eyelid jumped, it meant good luck.

A few days later when I came home from school, Ah Pau had brought home a small bundle of bamboo strips. They were about five or six feet long. Each strip was about a half inch wide and a quarter inch thick.

"What are the bamboo strips for, Ah Pau?"

"I'm going to teach you how to make chicken fences during the New Year holiday. If you're lucky enough, I think you can make enough money for the camping fee before the camp-out."

"Really? Why don't you teach me now? They seem easy to make and more fun than embroidery."

"You need to wait for the New Year holiday. I don't want it to interfere with your schoolwork."

"Oh, I wish tomorrow was New Year's. I can hardly wait, Ah Pau!"

"I know you are excited. But first, I have to ask Kee to thin the bamboo strips for you."

"I can do it myself!"

"No, it's too dangerous for you. You have to use a knife. I think Kee can handle it better than you."

When Kee came home, Ah Pau explained to him about making the chicken fences and asked him if he would help me thin the bamboo strips.

"What's the deal?"

"What deal?" I asked.

"You have to share your profit with me!"

"What do you mean?"

"I mean, I need to have my share."

"Oh, how much?"

"Hmmm . . . one-fourth."

"How much is that?"

"Well, if you earn forty cents, I will get ten cents."

"That's a lot!"

"Think about it, dummy! You are the one who needs the camp fee, not me. I will have it from your *lai see* money."

Kee was very good at blackmailing me. "Okay," I said unwillingly, but I was thinking that someday when I grew up, I would get even with him.

CHAPTER 7

On New Year's Eve it was cold outside, but warm and cozy inside.

Kee and I had planned to stay up all night to welcome the New Year. But I couldn't make it. When I woke up to the sound of loud fire-crackers outside, I was curled up at the end of the daybed with a cotton quilt on top of me. The whole living room was golden bright because the oil lamps, candles, and incense were all lit on the long worship table at the end of the living room. The whole house was filled with the fragrance of burning candles and incense.

"Is it New Year now?" I asked Ah Pau, who was kneeling down in front of the worship table.

"It is!" Ah Pau said.

I looked around and asked, "Where's Kee?"

"In his bed. He couldn't stay awake, either."

I jumped to the floor and ran across the living room to Kee's bed. I pulled open the mosquito net. "Hey, Kee! Get up!"

Kee opened his eyes, dazed for a few seconds.

"It's New Year now!"

"New Year? Oh!" At once, he jumped off his bed, put his fists together, and chanted to Ah Pau as loudly as he could, "*Kung hay fat choi*, Grandma!"

I also put my fists together and chanted, "*Kung hay fat choi*, Ah Pau!"

"Good boy. Good girl." Ah Pau at once pulled out two *lai see* money pockets from her *tong cheong sam* pocket and gave them to us, saying, "Grow up fast and be healthy!"

"Thank you. Thank you," we said in unison.

Uncle, Auntie, and Ah So came down from upstairs. We all said *Kung hay fat choi* to each other. Ah Pau gave *lai see* money to Uncle, saying, "Good business this year."

Uncle replied, "I hope you are as healthy and happy as always."

Ah Pau gave *lai see* to Auntie and wished, "I hope you have good health in this New Year."

Auntie said, "Same to you."

Then Ah Pau gave *lai see* to Ah So and said, "I hope this year you'll find a nice, rich husband."

Ah So was so shy that she lowered her head.

Then Uncle and Auntie gave *lai see* to Ah So, Kee, and me. They said to Kee and me, "We hope you both study hard and are promoted each year."

"Thank you," Kee and I answered.

I wanted to go back to my room to open the *lai see* pockets and see how much was inside, because it was very impolite to open presents in front of the person who gave it to you. But Kee demanded, "Hey! Give your *lai see* to me now!"

Uh-oh, he had his eyes on my *lai see* money already!

"Can I keep it a little longer, Kee?" I begged. "Without *lai see* in my pocket, it doesn't seem like New Year."

Kee was thinking. His nose was sniffling.

"You trust me, don't you?" I pleaded.

"All right, just this time."

"Thanks. By the way, do I have to go out every day to say *Kung hay fat choi* and get *lai see*? I want to start learning how to make chicken fences."

"You can go today, tomorrow, and the day after tomorrow."

"Day after tomorrow? You know not many people go visiting on the third day of New Year. If they see someone that day, they might quarrel with that person for the rest of the year."

"Okay," Kee said. "I'll let you get away with the third day. But you have to give me at least enough for the camp fee."

"What if I don't get enough the first couple of days?"

"You'll have to go on the fourth day."

"What? I won't have time to make chicken fences!"

"Who told you to borrow my junk for an apple? Do you regret it now?"

"Who said I regret it? I have never regretted it!"

"Don't argue! It's New Year!" Ah Pau reminded us.

Before we ate our twice-a-year breakfast, I lit up the kerosene lamp and put on my red cotton jacket and the *tong cheong* pants. Ah Pau made them for me just for the New Year.

"*Whaah!* The jacket is almost down to my knees, Ah Pau!"

Ah Pau smiled and admitted, "I made it a

little too big—even a pregnant woman could wear it."

"Look, the pants almost swallow me. See? They reach up to my chest. Why did you make them that big, Ah Pau?"

"So you can wear the outfit for several years. When I blink my eyes, you will have already grown into it." She helped me roll up the sleeves, and she quickly hemmed my pant legs so I could walk.

My shoes were even worse. They were black leather shoes that Ah Pau had asked one of my uncles to get for me all the way from Canton. They were so big that my feet almost disappeared inside them.

Ah Pau was very smart. She had already stuffed some leftover cotton from the jacket into my shoes.

"Let me help you tie the shoelaces so they won't drop off," Ah Pau said. She tied them as tightly as she could until I could walk.

"It's very clumsy to walk, Ah Pau."

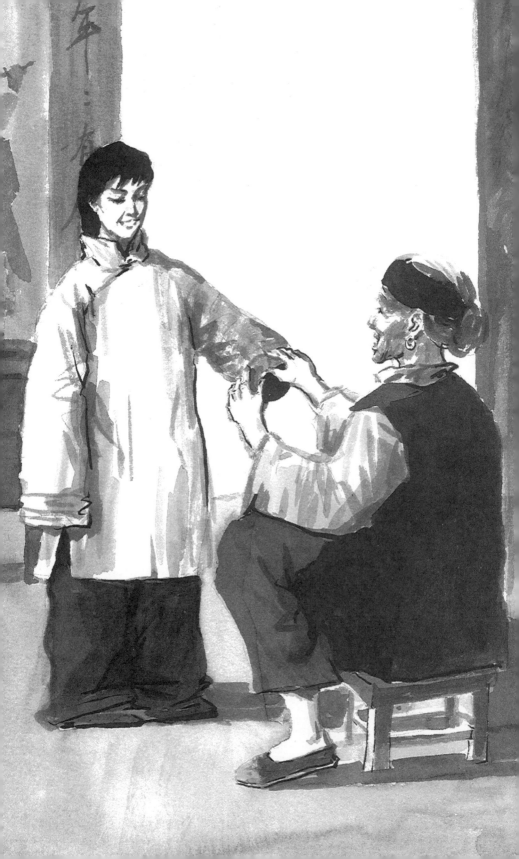

Ah Pau laughed. "You are so skinny. Eat more rice, and hurry to grow up so you can fit into your clothes!"

When I came out to the living room, Uncle and Auntie had their best clothes on. Not new, but best. Ah So, who was taking the special New Year food to the table, also had on her new light pink cotton jacket. It fit her very well. But poor Kee looked as if he were wearing Uncle's clothes.

"Look at the *leen go*, *jeen dui*, *yau gok*, and *jung*! I'm hungry. Let's eat!" Kee couldn't wait.

We all sat down at the table. I greeted the others by saying, "Ah Pau, eat. Uncle, eat. Auntie, eat. Ah So, eat. Kee, eat."

Kee just mumbled his greeting. Then Kee and I piled up food into our bowls. Because we had another important mission to do, Kee crammed food into his mouth so fast that he almost couldn't chew!

Pretty soon I couldn't stuff in anymore, but there was a lot of food still in my bowl. Ah Pau couldn't be mad at me because of New Year.

She just said, "Your eyes are bigger than your stomach."

Before we left the house, both Kee and I grabbed a big handful of *gwa gee* from a tray and put them into our pockets. I saw Auntie's eyes grow large in amazement. But she dared not say a word because of the New Year. I only heard Ah Pau warn us, "If you eat that many *gwa gee*, watch out! Your tongues will be sore."

CHAPTER 8

When we hobbled outside, the cold New Year air was full of the smell of gunpowder. In front of each house, fragments of red firecracker paper were scattered like a thick red carpet of flowers. Ah Mei, Ah Man, Ah Pui, Ah Tyim, Ah Wing, and other small children were all at the plaza. They were dressed in their once-a-year best clothes and their clumsy shoes, either too big or too small.

"Have you gone around to say *Kung hay fat choi?*" Kee asked Ah Man.

"We've been waiting for you," Ah Man said.

"Okay, let's go to Ah Tyim's house first," Kee said. He was always the leader when we were in a group.

Ah Tyim's house was right next to the narrow alley. It was the only exit from Chan Village to the outside because all thirteen of the gray brick two-story houses were arranged in a horseshoe shape.

No one closed front doors during the daytime in Chan Village because everyone was related. Just as we all swarmed into the courtyard, everyone chanted loudly, "*Kung hay fat choi!*" Then we entered Ah Tyim's house. Ah Tyim's grandpa and father happily gave away *lai see* money pockets, one by one, until everybody got four of them. Ah Tyim's grandma passed around a tray of *gwa gee* and special New Year sweets, like candied coconut, strips of winter melon, and sweet lotus seeds. We stuck our hands in and grabbed whatever we pleased and stuffed it into our pockets. Ah Tyim's mother offered us hot tea, but we didn't bother to take even one sip. Our New Year greeting was different from the grown-ups'. They would bring food to someone's house, then they would have tea and chat about the weather or about daily routines. But we didn't. Our greeting was to receive *lai see* money and get rich! So, as soon as we got the *lai see* and goodies, we left.

Before we entered another house, we were all anxious to open up the *lai see* pockets to see how much was inside.

"How much did you get?" Ah Mei asked me.

"One cent. How about you?" I said. I put the money in my pocket and threw the red money holder on the ground as everybody else did.

"The same," Ah Mei said. "I've got a total of four cents already. Not bad."

We discovered that all of us were getting the same amount. We were happy because we

were all being treated equally. I was especially pleased because I was the only one whose last name was Yeung instead of Chan.

We went door-to-door. My pockets were full of money and goodies, but my shoes were killing me. I was often the last one to get in and the last one to get out—until I took off my shoes and socks and left them at the plaza. Whew! My feet were finally free! I preferred to walk barefoot on the cold ground. I could walk or run as I pleased. When we finished getting *lai see* from all the houses, the plaza was littered with red *lai see* pockets as well as all our shoes, including Kee's!

We were ready to go to the intersection outside of Chan Village for snacks because we were all rich, even richer than the grown-ups. And there were three times as many snack stalls there as usual.

"Hey! Give it all to me now!" Kee said, keeping his eye on me.

I really didn't feel like letting all the *lai see* go. "Can I keep it a while longer?"

"You will spend it when you go outside."

"No, I won't."

"I may give you some back."

So I gave a handful of money to him. He counted it. It was twenty cents.

"Not so bad for just one day." Kee was very pleased. "You can have two cents for a snack."

"Oh, thanks. Free?"

"Well," Kee hesitated. "That means you only gave me eighteen cents instead of twenty."

"That means not free," I said. "No thanks. I want to go home and make chicken fences."

"But you still have to go out for *lai see* tomorrow."

"I know."

"Don't say that I didn't offer any money to you. Otherwise, Grandma will jump on me."

"I won't."

I picked up my shoes and went home, while he went off with the others.

After the second day, Kee decided I had paid him back enough. I was finally free from the debt I owed him.

On the third day of New Year, Kee learned how to thin the bamboo strips with a knife. Our living room was soon full of bamboo strips that almost tripped Ah Pau.

Just a couple of days before the new semester started, Ah Pau examined the chicken fences I had made and praised me. "I think your handwork is good enough for us to sell."

"Really?" I was thrilled.

Kee grabbed the chance and demanded, "I deserve one-half of her profits instead of one-fourth, Grandma. One-fourth is nothing!"

"What?" I couldn't believe my ears!

"I deserve one-half! See, she did the easy job, and I did the hard one! I carried the heavy strips home from the store and thinned them and smoothed them, and she just bent over and wove them!"

"Who says that I only did the easy job!" I defended myself, because weaving chicken fences was not as easy as what Kee described. "I have to bend down on the hard, cold floor, and it hurts my knees and back. Sometimes you don't smooth the strips so well, and the splinters stick into my fingers. Sometimes the strips hit me in the face. Do you remember the day before yesterday when a strip sprang up and hit me in the eye? I didn't do the easy job. You are just greedy, that's all!"

But Ah Pau was listening to us and said, "Well, this time I will not say Kee is trying to take advantage of you, Ying. You both have done an equal amount of work. So, Kee asking for an equal amount is fair."

Kee gave me a triumphant grin.

What could I say?

"How much can I get if I sell one?" I asked.

Ah Pau counted with her fingers. "One-half of the money has to pay for the materials. You and Kee can split the other half."

"How much can I sell a chicken fence for?"

"I don't know yet. It depends on the market price. But don't worry. Just work hard."

"All right," I said.

CHAPTER 9

"Do you have enough *lai see* for the camp fee?" Ming Ming asked me as I put my book-bag into my drawer in the first desk. We had come early because it was the first day of spring semester, the seventh day of New Year.

"Not yet, but I will. How about you?" I asked as Ming Ming walked toward my seat.

"Almost," she answered. Her seat was four desks behind mine. We had three rows of desks. Our row, which was on the left of the blackboard, was all girls except Ng Shing. The other two rows were boys. We had a total of forty-three students.

"I can hardly wait for the camp-out," I said."

"Me, either," said Ming Ming.

"Me, either," said Ping Ping. She and Ming Ming shared a desk.

"Do you have enough?" I asked her.

"Yes," Ping Ping said. "I only spent one cent of my *lai see* money. I tried very hard not to spend any of it."

Ah Mei came in. She sat two desks behind me. Before she put her bookbag into the drawer, Ming Ming asked her. "Are you still not planning to go, Ah Mei?"

"No, I'm not going," Ah Mei said.

"I wonder if Ah Mei is the only one not going," Ping Ping said.

"I don't think Cripple Yip will go." I said the name Cripple Yip very quietly because she was sitting on her bench all by herself, just behind mine. I didn't know how old she was, but she was very small. She had two pigtails reaching to her shoulders. But her hair looked dry, and it wasn't as black as ours. (Ah Pau said that kind of hair meant a lack of nutrition.) Her clothes were even worse than mine. They had patches mended on either the shoulders or the elbows or both. Her real name was Yip On, but we always called her Cripple Yip behind her back. She never played with us.

"Has she ever talked to you, Ying?" Ming Ming asked. She swung her two thick pigtails to her back.

"No," I said.

"I thought maybe she talked to you since you sit in front of her," Ming Ming said.

"Uh-uh," I said.

"How come she doesn't like to talk?" Ping Ping also lowered her voice, but her eyes were looking in Cripple Yip's direction.

"I don't know," I said. "Probably because she can't play with us."

"Does she still live with her grandma?" Ming Ming asked.

"I guess," I said.

"Where are her parents?"

"I don't know."

"Do you think her parents have died, and she came to live with her grandma?" asked Ping Ping. She was very curious.

"I don't know," I said.

The bell rang, and we all went back to our seats.

Ng Shing breezed into class. He plopped down on the bench noisily. The force was so great that he tilted Cripple Yip's desk and caused all her pencils and brushes to roll to the floor. He didn't say he was sorry, and Cripple Yip didn't say a word, either. She just picked up her pens. Just before Mrs. Yu, who had given birth to a girl again, came in, Ng Shing opened his pen box and bragged, "Look! I already have the camp money."

"So what! I'll have it, too, soon." I didn't really want to talk to him. I had lost an expensive apple because of him. After literature period was over, we ran outside for physical education. But on the way to the playground I tripped on a stump and twisted my ankle. It hurt so much, I sat on the ground and cried. Ah Mei informed Mr. Wong, our physical education teacher, who came over to check on me.

"Are you all right?" he asked.

"No, not really. . . . It hurts," I said.

He checked my right ankle and suggested, "Well, you may go back to your classroom to rest."

"Okay."

He pulled me up. Ah Mei offered to help me back to the class. After I hopped several steps, I told Ah Mei, "I can walk back by myself."

"You sure?" Mr. Wong asked.

"Yes."

So they both left me, and I limped back to the classroom.

As I was entering my room, someone almost ran into me. It was Cripple Yip. She was shuffling out of the classroom in a hurry. After that there was no one in the room but me.

At the beginning of third period—calligraphy—Ng Shing opened his pen box to get his brush. Suddenly he yelled, "Yeung Ying stole my money!"

"What?"

"You stole my money!"

"What's happening?" Mrs. Yu asked. She stared at us over the rims of her black-frame glasses.

"Yeung Ying stole my two *yuan*!"

"No, I didn't!"

"Both of you, stand up."

As I stood up, I heard the rest of my schoolmates murmuring.

"Class! Stop mumbling! Get back to your calligraphy." The class was quiet. Then Mrs.

Yu started to question Shing. "How much did you say you lost?"

"Two *yuan.*"

"Why did you have that much money at school?"

"My father gave it to me for the camp fee."

"It's too early to pay for the camp fee."

He didn't say anything.

"Where did you put your money?"

"Inside my pen box."

"Are you sure it's gone?"

"Yeah."

"Did anybody see the money in the pen box?"

"Nobody but Yeung Ying."

"How did she know?"

"I showed her."

"When?"

"At the beginning of first period."

"And you just now found out that it is missing?"

"Yeah."

"That means your money disappeared while you were in physical education?"

"Yes! But only Yeung Ying was in the class. Nobody would know but her."

"I didn't take his money. Cripple Yip was also in the class when I came in." I began to cry.

"Were you, Yip On?"

"Yes, ma'am."

"You stand up, too. Why were you in the classroom while everybody else was out?" Even though Mr. Wong gave permission for Yip On not to participate in any activity, she still had to be outside. Most of the time she just shuffled along the railing at the pond.

"I . . . I needed to go to the bathroom. I came in to get the toilet paper." Every student had to take his own toilet paper.

"Did you get permission from Mr. Wong?"

"No. I could barely wait, and he was busy with Yeung Ying."

Then Mrs. Yu asked me why I had to go inside the class. I told her.

She asked Cripple Yip, "Then you got the toilet paper and went straight to the bathroom?"

"Yes, ma'am."

"Was there anybody else in the class when you came in?"

"No, ma'am, but Yeung Ying was coming in when I rushed to the bathroom."

"Well, both of you open your bookbags."

I put my bookbag on the desk. She searched it thoroughly, even checking inside my books. Then she searched my desk, and even my clothes. I felt like running away, far, far away where nobody was. Shing gave me a "see-how-you-can-get-away" look while Mrs. Yu searched me. She searched Cripple Yip, too, but found nothing. Then Mrs. Yu ordered the whole class to take out their bookbags and exchange them to search, except for Shing. He felt he was special. Yuck!

Nothing was found. Finally Mrs. Yu declared, "Yeung Ying and Yip On, both of you are suspects. I will give two days for whoever stole the money to admit it without punishment. Otherwise, if I find out who stole it, that person will have to see the principal. Do you understand?"

"Yes," I whispered and started to cry again.

After class, Ng Shing, Chan Wing, and some other boys called me a thief. Ming Ming, Ping Ping, and other girls didn't call me a name, but when I went to the playground later on to join them in jump rope, they all ran away from me, including Ah Mei.

At supper that evening, I didn't feel like eating. In my mind I was wondering, "What if I need to see the principal?" I had never been to see the principal since I started school.

Ah Pau noticed my unusual mood. She put her bony hand on my forehead and asked, "Are you sick?"

"No," I said.

"You don't feel as if you have a fever," Ah Pau said, taking her hand away from my forehead.

Kee announced, "She's lovesick! I've seen her write a secret note to Mr. Hon!"

"Shut up!" Tears started pouring down my cheeks. It startled Ah Pau. Then I told her how Ng Shing showed me the two *yuan*, how I twisted my ankle, and how Mrs. Yu searched me in front of the class. Ah Pau did not seem to care about Shing's money, but she said, "Let me see your foot."

I showed my right foot to her. She held it and examined it. "It looks a little swollen. I am going to massage in some medicine for you."

After supper Ah Pau took the *teet da jow* and started to rub it on my right ankle. While she was doing that, she said, "You don't need to be upset over the money as long as you know you did not do anything wrong. Time will prove who is the thief and who is not. You just forget about it and try to put your mind at ease."

I felt much better because Ah Pau knew me well. She trusted me and understood me.

CHAPTER 10

The third day after Ng Shing lost his money, Mrs. Yu rushed into the class without a smile on her face. She asked, "Shing, was your two-*yuan* bill new or old?"

"It was new."

Mrs. Yu opened her grade book and took out a two-*yuan* bill and handed it back to Shing. "From now on, don't bring any money to school. Understand?"

Then she stared at me through her glasses. "A boy in the second grade accidentally found it under a rock behind his classroom. What are you going to say, Yeung Ying and—"

Someone cried out behind me.

"*You* did it, didn't you?" Mrs. Yu asked Yip On, very surprised.

"I'm sorry," Cripple Yip cried.

"Stand up, Yip On!" Mrs. Yu ordered. I was afraid to look at Mrs. Yu. She was very mad. Then she ordered again, "Class, read all the banners on both sides of the room! Read from the left side first!"

There were three banners on both sides of the room. They were written in big black characters on red pieces of paper. But the red color had faded to orange. We all recited as loudly as we could:

"Be an honest student!"

"Don't lie!"

"Don't steal!"

Then we read those on the right side of the wall:

"Don't be afraid to confess if you do something wrong!"

"Study hard every day!"

"Do exercise every day!"

"Thank you, class." Then she turned back to Cripple Yip. "What do you have to say? I thought you were a very good student. You have disappointed me—you lied to me. I have already given you two days, but you didn't confess. Go see the principal!" Then Mrs. Yu rapidly wrote something on a piece of paper and waved it in the air. "Take this with you!"

I had never thought that Cripple Yip would steal the money. When Ng Shing accused me, I defended myself by just telling the truth—I was not the only one in the class. I didn't mean to turn her in. I felt very bad. Therefore, I dared not turn back to see her until she dragged herself from her seat, got the paper, and hobbled out of the classroom. That was the first time I really noticed the way she limped. It was very pitiful because the bottom of her right foot was turned inward and her right ankle almost touched the ground. Every time she raised her right leg, she had to bend sideways and put her hand on her knee to support herself. I suddenly felt very sorry for her. What punishment would she get from the principal? Would he beat her other leg so she couldn't walk at all? I was worried.

Fortunately, Cripple Yip hobbled back to our classroom at about the middle of the next period. I felt much better because her left leg was all right. But she must have been spanked because her big round eyes looked very sad and she had been crying hard. When she sat back in her seat, she was still sniffling and sucking in air. I wanted to tell her that I was sorry, but I couldn't get the words out.

That afternoon when I got back home, I said to Ah Pau, "Do you know who stole the money?"

"Who?"

"Yip On, the crippled girl."

Ah Pau didn't ask me who Yip On was, but I saw a smile on her square, wrinkled face. "See,

I told you that you didn't need to be upset."

I said quietly, "She got spanked. I could tell."

"She stole. She deserved it! If she didn't get any punishment now, she might end up in jail later."

"But she's crippled."

"That doesn't make stealing all right."

"You don't understand, Ah Pau. She looked very sad," I said. I suddenly felt that she was not my Ah Pau—she was a stranger—because my Ah Pau always had a kind heart for other people.

The next morning on the way to school, I bought a tube of spicy dried beans and ate about half the tube. Then I left the rest for Cripple Yip. I wanted to show her how sorry I was. But Cripple Yip was not in class first period, so I put the half tube of dried beans into her desk drawer. By the time school was out, she still was not there. I wondered why she hadn't come to school—she had never missed school before.

CHAPTER 11

*C*ripple Yip didn't show up in class for two days, but I didn't take back the dried beans. Instead, I added a dried salty plum, and I hid it at the back of the drawer in her desk so nobody would steal it.

On the third day, Cripple Yip still had not shown up. I asked Ah Mei during recess, "Do you know why Cripple Yip is not coming to school?"

"I guess she was suspended," Ah Mei said, ready to jump rope.

"Why?"

"She stole, remember?"

"I know . . . but how come Chung Kong in fifth grade is still in school? He stole several times last year, remember?"

"I don't know. I think I saw her this morning." Ah Mei tripped. She handed the rope to me and said, "Your turn now."

"Where did you see her?"

Ah Mei said, "I think on the way to school. I thought she was going to school, too."

Too bad I didn't see her, I thought. Then I would tell her that I had something for her.

I was very good at jumping rope. I could always jump more than three hundred times before I missed. But this time, I only made it to one hundred and one and tripped. My mind was not on jumping rope.

The bell rang. We all were ready to return

to our classroom. Suddenly there was a shout. "Someone is drowning!"

"Someone is drowning!" more students yelled.

"Where? Where?" someone asked.

"Over at the broken dam!"

A white figure rushed past me. It was Mr. Hon, a new teacher who had come from Canton. He taught fifth-grade Chinese literature. He rushed toward the broken dam, which was about one hundred and fifty feet from us. The principal and other male teachers also ran towards the dam.

We ran to the brick railing to look. The railing was built along the playground to prevent students from falling into the pond next to the school. But I couldn't see anything until Mr. Hon dove right into the cold water beside the broken dam. Then I spotted something small— it was thin and silver—in the water. It shone in the late morning sun.

Someone blew a whistle. With a ruler in her hand, Mrs. Yu chased us back to the classrooms.

"Who was it?" everybody asked, but nobody knew.

No one paid attention to Mrs. Yu. No one followed the lessons she ordered us to read aloud, especially Ng Shing and the students who were seated next to the two windows. When Mrs. Yu wandered to the back of the class and peered outside, Shing stood up and looked out the window toward the dam.

"Do you see anything?" I asked.

"No, the water is too low. But there are more people running to look."

"Do you see Mr. Hon?"

"I told you, the water is too low, dummy!"

I crossed my fingers and hoped Mr. Hon and whoever was drowning were okay.

"There's Mr. Hon! He's dragging somebody!" a student at the back of the classroom suddenly exclaimed. We all rushed toward the back windows facing the pond. Mrs. Yu didn't stop us. She also rushed to look. She asked anxiously, "Is it a child?"

"Can't tell," someone said.

A big crowd of people gathered near the broken earth dam. Through the crowd, I spotted a white figure bending down. It must be Mr. Hon, I thought. He looked like he was doing something to try to save the person.

I held my breath, but my left eyelid jumped rapidly. I rubbed it several times to make it stop. I hoped something bad was not going to happen.

Then I saw Mr. Hon stand up very slowly. His head was down.

The whole class was quiet—the person must be dead.

None of us moved. No one made a sound. A few minutes later there was a knock on the door. It was the principal.

"Class . . . ," he announced.

"Oh, no." I trembled all over when I heard his words.

I wished the announcement was a terrible mistake.

I wished it was just a nightmare.

I felt sick. I wanted to go home.

CHAPTER 12

*T*hat night, I had a terrible bad dream. I screamed in the middle of the night, "Run! Run!"

Someone shook me and said, "You are having a nightmare again."

When I opened my eyes, I could tell that it was Ah Pau next to me in the dark. I could feel my heart beating very fast.

"I dreamed I was in a jungle and—"

"Wait, eat a little something first," Ah Pau interrupted me. She turned the kerosene lamp brighter and hurriedly left the room with the lamp. When she returned, she had a cup of hot tea and a spoonful of cold rice with her. I ate the rice and drank the tea. Otherwise, the bad dream would come true. "Okay, you can tell me now."

"I was in a jungle. I was tricking Cripple Yip. I said, 'Hey, Cripple Yip, come and get the candy!' so she hopped around to where I was. Before she came to me, I hid behind a tree so she had to look for me again. Suddenly all the trees turned into wild wolves. They were circling Cripple Yip. I tried to save her, but I couldn't run fast enough, and the wolves were tearing Cripple Yip apart."

Ah Pau embraced me and said, "Just try not to think about the dream, okay?"

But I still couldn't sleep; I was afraid to close my eyes. Every time I did, I could see Cripple Yip hobbling clumsily to see the principal. Ah Pau stayed up with me all night long.

The next day I didn't go to school. I was very tired. Ah Pau sighed and said, "She should have known that it was the third year. . . ."

"She probably didn't know that the water ghost was looking for someone this year. She just came here last semester."

"She was unlucky, that's all. I'm going to give her spirit some food, clothes, and money and let it be satisfied, so it can go home and leave you alone." Ah Pau helped me hook back the mosquito net and then went out and bought some colored paper clothes, paper clogs, paper fish, and hell money. She burned all of it near the broken dam where Cripple Yip drowned.

I couldn't go to school the next day, either. I felt like the inside of my heart was falling apart. Sometimes my heart seemed to be floating everywhere and it couldn't settle down as it was supposed to. I was afraid to be alone. Ah Pau said, "You are being scared to death. I'm going to buy some *ju sax* and a pig heart to cook soup for you. It's the best thing for a person who has had a serious fright."

But I didn't want to be alone, so she brought my pillow and quilt and let me lie on the daybed in the living room. She waited until Kee came home from school, then she went out.

Kee was very kind to me when he wasn't trying to take advantage of me, bossing me, or when I didn't feel well. "Want to read these?" He handed me the comic books that he had checked out from school. He started to do his homework on the table next to the daybed.

Suddenly I burst into tears for the first time. "It's all my fault. If I didn't turn her in that day, she wouldn't have needed to see the principal, she wouldn't have been suspended from school, and then . . ."

"What are you talking about?" Kee asked. He had just written down the title for a composition on a piece of paper. "She got suspended not because of stealing, but because she owed the

school for her tuition. She didn't even pay for last semester."

"How do you know?"

"*Aiyah!* Don't you ever look at the bulletin board in front of the teacher's office? There were four more students besides her who were suspended. It said they couldn't come back until they paid all their tuition. I don't know what you do at school not to keep up with what's going on."

"You really mean it?"

"The notice is still there. If you don't believe me, you can go see for yourself. . . . Girls—they don't keep up with anything!"

I let out a deep sigh for the first time since Cripple Yip's death.

I said, "If I had known that she would drown, I would never have said that she was coming out of the classroom when I came in."

"How come you have such a tender heart suddenly, huh? You didn't say she stole it, did you? It was she who admitted it."

"But—still . . ."

"Besides that, she didn't get suspended because of stealing. You shouldn't blame that on yourself. It'll drive you crazy. Do you want to have a nervous breakdown?"

"What does that mean?"

"It means go crazy. Do you want that?"

I shook my head.

"Then try not to think about it. It wasn't your fault."

"Whose fault was it?"

"I don't know." He tapped the pencil on the table. "Probably hers. She broke the school rule—nobody is allowed to go there, remember?"

"Ah Pau said the dead fish was a lure."

"A lot of people said that, too. You were very lucky that the *sahng yu* was not a lure."

I felt cold all over.

"She shouldn't have tried to get the dead fish," Kee said.

"Maybe she did it for food. I saw her and her grandmother picking up discarded yellow vegetable leaves once. She probably stole Ng

Shing's money for food, too."

"Maybe—or maybe to pay for her school tuition—or maybe to pay for the camp fee—or maybe she was just greedy."

"Not to pay for the camp fee—she never would have gone."

"I know whose fault it was—it was because she was poor."

"But you just said it was her fault."

"See, if they were not so poor, she wouldn't have owed the school for her tuition and gotten suspended. So being poor was the main cause of her death."

"Do you think so?"

"Sure. Don't talk to me now. I have to write at least five hundred words for this stupid essay."

He wrote about ten words, but erased them and bit his thumbnail, thinking.

A few minutes later, I had another question. "What will happen to her grandma now?"

"She'll mourn and be heartbroken for sure."

"She's all by herself now," I said very quietly.

I thought about the old beggar that Ah Pau took pity on. After a while, I said, "You know what?" I knew Kee would prefer to answer my question than do the essay. He hated compositions—he hated literature, just the opposite of me. "I want to say I'm sorry to her."

"But you don't know her, and she doesn't know you."

"I know." I was a little discouraged. "Do you think she will die, too?"

"Everybody will die sooner or later."

"I mean die from being lonely."

"I don't know about that."

"Will she die from being poor?"

"Maybe. But I think she will find some way to survive."

"How?"

"I don't know."

"You know what, Kee? I wish I was rich so I could give all the money to her."

"You're dreaming again. You will never get rich—you're not the rich type."

"How do you know? Maybe tomorrow I

will find a bunch of money on the ground."

"Hey! You've bothered me for almost half an hour, and I haven't written twenty words! Would you leave me alone now?"

"I'm sorry."

Later, I drank all the pig-heart-and-*ju sax* soup and ate the whole pig heart. My heart didn't feel as if it were floating anymore. Ah Pau was glad. She said, "I think you can go back to school tomorrow."

CHAPTER 13

*T*he third day after Cripple Yip's death, I went back to school. As I went in, I saw that all the seats were moved around. "Hey, where is my seat?" I cried out.

"Mrs. Yu switched all the desks and benches to the other direction. She even changed the blackboard," said Ah Mei.

"And she moved the spittoon, too," Ping Ping chimed in. The spittoon had been at the front right corner, but now it had also been moved to the other end.

"Why did she switch everything all around?" I asked.

"I don't know why, but people often do that when there is a death," Ping Ping said.

I looked carefully. Cripple Yip's desk and bench were gone. I wondered if anybody had found the food that I had left for her. I wished I had given it to her earlier. I wished I had talked with her before.

All through the day, nobody mentioned Cripple Yip's name. It seemed that she had never been in the classroom. I felt very sad. Suddenly I wanted to see her grandma. When school was out, I asked Ah Mei, "Would you please go to see Cripple Yip's grandma with me?"

"Are you kidding?" Her big round eyes opened wide. Even though she was eleven and I was ten, I thought she was not as brave as I was.

"No, I'm not."

"Do you know Cripple Yip's spirit is still around her house?" After she died, her spirit would wander around her home for one hundred days because she still didn't want to part from her family. That's why we had several ceremonies during the first hundred days after a family member's death.

"So?"

"Aren't you scared?"

"We can take some weeping willow sticks with us to keep the spirits away."

"But . . . what are you going there for?"

"I don't know . . . I just want to see her grandma, I guess."

"Why? What are you going to do when you see her?"

"I want to tell her I'm sorry."

"But she doesn't know you."

"I know. I'll tell her that I was Cripple Yip's schoolmate."

"So?"

"And I have one cent for her. I didn't have time to buy a snack this morning."

Ah Mei laughed. "One cent! One cent for us can buy a slice of sweet potato or a banana, but one cent for a grown-up is nothing!"

I felt very stupid. I said, "But it is all I have."

"Don't be so silly, Ying."

Maybe Ah Mei was right. She was a year older than me, and she knew more stuff than I did. That's why Ah Pau always trusted her. But I still wanted to go. I begged, "Would you please go with me just this one time?"

"No, I don't want to."

"*Pleeease.* Remember last time I had a fever, but you still wanted me to look for beads with you in the theater. I sneaked out of the house and went, and Ah Pau was so mad at me. Remember?"

"Well . . . Okay. But I can't stay long."

"You'll go?"

"But you have to get the weeping willow sticks first."

So I sneaked behind the teacher's dormitory and cautiously broke off two weeping willow sticks from a tree. I let Ah Mei hold one, and I held the other—to get rid of the spirits.

Cripple Yip's grandma lived at Nam Sar. It was south of Tai Kong, about three miles from our school. We knew her house, which was at the side of a dirt road, because we saw Cripple Yip there when we passed by to collect pine straw for fuel on Buddhist Hill. It was a tiny old farmer's hut, made out of mud and hay. On one side of the hut was a chicken coop; on the other was a small vegetable patch. When we got there, the old wooden door was closed. A couple of chickens were scratching around the vegetable patch in which the grandma had grown lettuce. But the lettuce looked as if it were dying.

"You want to knock on the door?" Ah Mei asked me.

Suddenly I lost my courage. "Just wait a minute," I told her. So we wandered around the dirt road and waited for the door to open, but about a half hour later, the door was still closed.

"I have to go," Ah Mei said.

"Just wait a little longer."

"No. Why don't you knock on the door?"

"Just wait."

"What if she's out? We're just wasting time."

She was right; we got ready to leave. Just then we heard the door hinges creak. "Wait," I told Ah Mei. I saw Cripple Yip's grandma with a black bandanna on her head to keep warm. She shuffled out a couple of feet from the wooden door. My heart suddenly beat very fast.

"There she is!" Ah Mei poked me in the ribs. But my heart was still jumping hard, and my feet didn't want to move. I watched her put out a dish pan on the ground as the chickens all scurried to it. Then she closed the door again.

"Why did you just stand here!" Ah Mei's voice was not as gentle as usual.

"I don't know. It's hard to say 'I'm sorry' to her."

"I don't understand, Ying. I have to go."

"Please wait, Ah Mei."

"No, I have to go. I have a lot of homework."

"Well, okay." I started following Ah Mei

home, disappointedly. Then I suddenly called to her, "Wait a minute!"

"What?"

Without explaining to Ah Mei, I ran back to where the dish pan was and placed the one cent underneath it.

"You're weird, Ying."

"I don't care what you say. That's all I want to do."

CHAPTER 14

*E*arly one Sunday morning, while I was still lazily lying in bed, Ah Pau said, "The first spring farmers' market will be held in our town in about six weeks. It'll sell the most. If you want to have money for the camp-out, you'd better hurry and catch up. You've done only two fences so far."

"Do you know yet how much I can sell them for?"

"Yes. You can sell one fence for eighty cents."

"That means . . ."

Ah Pau said, "For each fence you can get twenty cents, after paying for the materials and giving Kee his portion."

"So I need to make"—I was counting in my head—"eight more fences in less than two months."

"That's why I told you to hurry up," Ah Pau said.

"Can I work on school days after I finish my homework?" Ah Pau only allowed me to work on Saturday afternoon and Sunday. She was afraid that I would ignore my schoolwork.

"Well," Ah Pau mumbled, "you seem absentminded recently. It may be good for you to have something to keep you busy."

So I wove chicken fences as often as I could. Our living room was always so littered with bamboo strips that we almost couldn't get through. Therefore, I didn't have time to

think too much about Cripple Yip's death. Pretty soon I had woven eight.

"Whew! Slow down," Kee said, looking at the untouched bundle of bamboo strips lying on the floor. "I can't keep up with you. I haven't even started thinning this bundle yet."

Auntie was amazed at my speed. She praised me. "Your little fingers are as fast as the wind."

Ah Pau said with a smile, showing her missing teeth in the front, "I am glad she knows how to weave chicken fences. At least she has a skill for living and will not starve to death."

By the night before the farmers' market, I had made a total of eleven chicken fences and was exhausted.

"Now, you just pray for good luck tomorrow," Ah Pau said. "If you can sell all of them, you will have a little money left over for snacks."

I didn't pray, because I was so tired that I dropped onto my bed and fell fast asleep.

It seemed as if I had just been asleep for a few minutes when Ah Pau woke me up. "Ugh," I mumbled and turned over.

"It is five minutes after four." Ah Pau pushed me gently and reminded me, "We have to get a good place so you can sell all your chicken fences."

I tumbled out of bed and rubbed my eyes. Then I washed my face with cold water. I was completely awake then. "Where is Kee? Isn't he up yet?"

"He's in the outhouse. He stayed up all night—he has diarrhea."

"Did you tie up the two big rolls of chicken fences for me, Ah Pau?"

"Yes," Ah Pau said. "Last night you were so tired."

"Thanks, Ah Pau. You're so nice. You even put the bamboo pole on them so they're ready to carry."

I tried to put the bamboo pole on my shoulder to carry them, but they were too heavy.

"I don't think you can carry them," Ah Pau said. "You may be able to carry Ah So's baby hats." There was a bundle of Ah So's embroidered baby hats lying on the floor. She and Auntie were out of town for a few days, so Ah Pau had to help her sell the hats.

"You did so much, Ah Pau. Did you go to bed at all?"

"I'm not sleepy," Ah Pau said. "I am very excited about the sale."

"Me, too."

Kee came back inside from the outhouse, looking pale and tired.

"Feeling a little better?" Ah Pau asked.

"I guess," Kee said.

"You both eat something before we start," Ah Pau said. She poured hot tea from a container into two bowls of cold rice to warm the rice. It took too long to start a fire in our clay stove.

"I don't feel like eating, Grandma," Kee said.

"I don't, either," I said.

"Well, I'm afraid you both will be hungry," Ah Pau said. But she did not insist we eat this time. I could tell she wanted to start our mission, and so did I.

"Let's go," I said.

Kee squatted down and balanced both of the bundles of chicken fences on his shoulders. Then he stood straight up. It did not look heavy for him at all.

I carried the baby hats and Ah Pau's small stool that Kee made for her.

Ah Pau took an old sheet to spread out on the ground and a small bundle of dried sea grass. "Let's go," she said.

Kee started toward the door. I waited for Ah Pau. She blew out the kerosene lamp. It was dark. I helped Ah Pau so she wouldn't trip in the dark. We closed the door behind us.

"Oh, the ground is cold!" I shivered. We were not wearing any shoes. The fresh, crisp spring chill spread all the way to my heart from the bottom of my feet!

"After walking for a while, you'll warm up," Ah Pau said.

The sky was still dark. The street lights were turned off after ten in the evening.

"Whew, so many people already!" I said.

"Of course. You want to get a good spot—

they want to, also," Ah Pau said.

I couldn't recognize the people's faces because of the dark, but I could tell many of them were carrying goods on their shoulders just like Kee. Some were carrying things on their backs, and others pushed homemade carts. Everybody was rushing to go in the same direction, south of town, where the farmers' market was being held. It was about two-and-a-half miles from Chan Village.

I liked to go to the farmers' market because it was only held a few times during spring and fall. The whole town seemed to go there. I didn't care as much as Ah Pau and other grown-ups about the prices or the freshness of the products. I just liked to play around, the way Kee and Ah Man did. Sometimes I liked to follow Ah So and her friends because they did not buy, either. They just looked to see who was the handsomest young man there, then Ah So and her friends would giggle at each other.

"Look, Ah Pau! There are so many lights

over there already! They look like long curved dragons."

"Of course. They are far ahead of us."

"Why didn't we bring a lamp with us, too?"

"Our stuff is simple," Ah Pau said, as she caught up with me. "By the time we get there, the sky will be turning light."

"Can you hear the baby chicks and ducks and the little pigs, Ah Pau? They sound like they are having a contest this morning."

"They sure do," Ah Pau said.

"Mmmm," I breathed greedily. "I can smell the fried rice cakes and carrot cakes. I'm hungry, Ah Pau."

"Your nose is as good as a dog's." Ah Pau laughed. Then she turned and looked for Kee. "Are you tired? You are walking slower than us."

"I'm all right," Kee said.

"So, hurry! I'm afraid we'll be late," I said.

When we finally got there, it was nearly dawn.

"It's three times as big as it used to be," Ah Pau said.

"My eyes are so confused, Ah Pau."

"Mine, too," Ah Pau mumbled. We were standing between two rows. "I don't know which row I want to take."

Some of the vendors were already laying their goods out on the ground. Some of them displayed their products in baskets or within their carts. Others still carried things on their shoulders and hadn't decided which row they would go to. Some of them said, "Excuse me, let me through," because they were not able to move through the crowd.

"Whew! My ears are going to be deaf," I said. I wanted to cover my ears, but I couldn't because my hands were so full. The noise from the baby chicks, geese, and ducks was much louder than before. The animals were all in cages, scattered among different stalls. They seemed to be competing to see which could make the loudest noise.

"They are as excited as we are," Ah Pau said. She was looking around. "I don't know which one will be the best."

Ah Pau believed that a good location would bring good luck.

I saw a middle-aged lady just putting down two baskets of plums in the row to our left. I loved to eat plums, so I jumped behind the lady, calling out, "Ah Pau, Kee, here!"

Ah Pau seemed hesitant to come. But Kee managed to get through the people and came to where I was. At once, he dumped the fences on the ground and said, "Right here. I have to find a place to go."

Ah Pau understood what he meant. She hurried to us and instructed Kee, "Go home and take some *Po Chai* pills. Ying and I can handle it."

Kee ran and promised her at the same time, "I will."

After Kee left, I said to Ah Pau, "Ah Pau, right here, next to the plums."

But Ah Pau was not very sure. "Wait a minute," she said.

Then she saw the man who was behind us put his two cages of baby ducks on the ground. He took the space beside us. Ah Pau whispered, "Just here, next to him."

"Let me spread out the sheet, Ah Pau," I said.

She untied the bundles of chicken fences from the bamboo pole and arranged the baby hats one by one from small size to large size.

"Are you going to spread out the chicken fences, too, Ah Pau?"

"No. They'll take up too much room." She put the two rolls of fences on the left. I put the bundle of dried sea grass on the sheet between Ah Pau and me.

"Ah Pau, you sit down." I put the stool behind her.

"Oh, I don't need to sit. I just want to look before the customers come." Ah Pau was very excited, I could tell.

I looked around, too. Right next to the

noisy baby ducks was a man placing carved wooden dolls, elephants, and turtles neatly on the ground on top of a red sheet. Directly in front of us was an old lady about Ah Pau's age who was selling candles and incense. To her right was an old man selling hand-painted chopsticks. Next was a person with a big bamboo hat, selling chickens in a cage. But about a couple of stalls from the big-bamboo-hat person was the fried-carrot-cake cart. Oh, it was the one that got all my attention because the fragrance of the fried cakes made me keep sniffing.

Ah Pau said to me, "This is a good spot."

"I hope you are right, Ah Pau. I want to sell *all* of my chicken fences."

"You will. Trust me."

"I do trust you, Ah Pau."

Ah Pau smiled at me and said, "Let me sit down to wait for our first customer."

I squatted down next to her.

CHAPTER 15

As soon as Ah Pau sat down, she coached me. "Whenever people come by, say, 'Good morning. Please look at the baby hats and chicken fences. The handwork is excellent. The chicken fences are strong and sturdy, but the price is fair. It's a good bargain.'"

"I already know that, Ah Pau," I teased her.

"Don't forget, I have watched you sell before?"

Ah Pau was so happy. The wrinkles on her square face seemed to have disappeared. She admitted, "I'm so excited. I know today is going to be our big day. Here . . ." Suddenly she whispered to me, "Look at that lady. She may buy one of your chicken fences."

"How do you know?"

"Don't ask. Keep a smile on your face."

I did. Because this time I was not just looking, but selling my own stuff. There was a grand-mother with a five- or six-year-old boy; she was squatting down and looking at the baby ducks next to us. I heard the grandmother say to the boy, "Want to raise some duck-ducks?"

The boy said, "Yes, I like duck-duck." So the grandmother bought four baby ducks. The man put some dry straw into her basket and placed the ducks inside.

Ah Pau quickly poked me. Just as the lady stood up, Ah Pau said happily to the boy, "Good morning. How are you? You're a nice-looking young boy. Your grandma bought you some ducks, huh? Might you need one of our chicken fences to keep your baby ducks from running away?"

The grandmother stopped and looked at the chicken fences. "How much are they?"

"One *yuan* apiece. Look," Ah Pau said. "They are very sturdy."

The lady examined the chicken fences. Ah Pau lowered her voice as if telling the grandmother a secret. "Since you are our first customer and I hope you can bring us good luck for the rest of the day, I'll sell one to you for just eighty cents, barely enough to cover the cost of the materials. But don't let anyone else know that I sold one to you for that price. Otherwise, they'll say I am not fair."

"How big are they?"

"About three feet by ten feet."

"Okay, give me one."

It was so easy! Ah Pau was a very good saleslady. I hurriedly untied one for her.

"I can tie some sea grass around it for you," Ah Pau said to me after I rolled up the one that I had just taken out.

"Thank you," Ah Pau said to the lady as she handed the money to Ah Pau and left.

I told Ah Pau, "I want to keep that money. It's *my* money."

"Put it in your pocket. Otherwise, your hard work will be for nothing."

"I will."

"Why didn't you say anything a while ago?"

"You didn't give me a chance, Ah Pau."

"Oh, I'm sorry. I was just so excited. . . . Good morning! What a beautiful hairdo you have!" Ah Pau said to a lady rice farmer. She had a newly fixed hairdo that was different from our town ladies'. She carried a bamboo pole with a coil of rope at the end of it. It meant she was going to shop for a lot of things.

The lady stopped when she heard Ah Pau complimenting her hairdo. With her farmer's dialect, she asked, "How much for the baby hats?"

Ah Pau whispered, "I'll give you a bargain. I'm supposed to sell them for two *yuan* for large ones, one *yuan* fifty cents for medium,

and one *yuan* for small. But I'll lower the price fifty cents. How about that?"

The farm lady chose one large and two small. "How much for them?"

Ah Pau mumbled for a while and replied, "Two fifty."

I also counted in my head. She was right, two *yuan* and fifty cents. Ah Pau couldn't read or write, but she could count very well. The lady farmer pointed to my chicken fences, asking, "How much for them?"

"Eighty cents apiece."

The lady didn't even check to see the handwork. She simply said, "Give me four. Oh, are they usual size?"

"Yes. Three by ten feet."

Four! I couldn't believe my ears! Ah Pau was so thrilled, she couldn't close her mouth!

We untied four of them. The farmer lady said, "Please divide them into two bundles. I'll carry them on my shoulder."

"Of course," Ah Pau said. After we fixed

everything for her, Ah Pau said to the lady, "Thank you. That will be five *yuan* and seventy cents all together."

The farmer lady took out a black handkerchief in which she had wrapped her money, and gave six *yuan* to Ah Pau. Ah Pau gave her change and said, "Have a good crop again!"

"Thank you," the farmer lady replied. She hoisted the bamboo pole to her shoulder and wandered over to another stand.

"Give that three *yuan* and twenty cents to me, Ah Pau."

Ah Pau exclaimed, "Can't believe it, huh? I told you that we would have a good day!"

"I want to just sell chicken fences for a living when I grow up," I told Ah Pau. Ah Pau didn't say anything; she just smiled.

For the next few hours, we were busy without a break. Finally I only had one chicken fence left, and there were still three of Ah So's baby hats.

"I want to count my money," I told Ah Pau.

But Ah Pau stopped me. "You'd better not;

you already know how much you have made."

"I still want to count it," I insisted. I had never had that much money in my pocket before. "I want to straighten out the bills."

Ah Pau gave me an "I-know-you-well" smile. "I know you want to play with your money, don't you? You'd better hurry to do that."

So I took out all the bills, spread them on the sheet, and straightened out each one. Then I divided the money into three groups and said, "This pile is for the materials, this one is for me, and this is for Kee. I have enough for the camp fee. If I can sell the last one, I can have money for snacks."

Ah Pau warned me, "You'd better put the money back now. You can see a person's face, but you can't see his heart."

So I quickly put all the money back into my pocket and declared, "I hope I can sell that last one soon."

"Don't worry, you will. Just do what you did a while ago—you did a good job."

CHAPTER 16

"*A*h Pau, how come nobody is stopping now?"

"You are nervous, aren't you?"

"More people are leaving now. What if I can't sell this one?"

"Just do what you did a while ago, and tell yourself you can sell it," Ah Pau encouraged me.

So I tried hard, much harder than before, to meet the people's eyes when they passed by, but they were not interested because the few items looked like leftovers to them. I kept saying, "What if nobody buys the last one, Ah Pau?"

"Don't worry. Someone will try to get one last bargain."

"I hope so," I said, looking around. The man who was selling ducks had sold all of them and was getting ready to leave.

I crossed my fingers and hoped that someone would buy the last chicken fence. Ah Pau blocked the sun's rays with her hand and said, "Oh, no wonder I am so hungry. The sun is right on top of our heads now. Are you hungry?"

"Yes! I'm very hungry. But I don't want to go home now. I want to sell my chicken fence first. Can I have a piece of carrot cake?"

"Sure. Go ahead and buy a couple," she said. Then she teased me, showing her missing front teeth. "You're rich now. You can afford to buy one for yourself."

"No, I'm not hungry."

"You're so stingy," she laughed. "Here, buy

three. I want to buy one for Kee."

I really didn't want to leave my stand—I was afraid I would miss the chance to sell the last chicken fence. Ah Pau seemed to see through me and said, "You go. I will try to sell it for you."

Before I left I told Ah Pau, "You can really lower the price, Ah Pau. I'm afraid I will not have any snack money."

Ah Pau laughed. "You're worried, huh? Let's wait and see."

I quickly left our space, hoping to get back soon. As I was about to get to the cake stand, someone said to me weakly, "Buy the big hen." I looked aside and almost cried out. It was Cripple Yip's grandma with the big bamboo hat! My heart suddenly beat fast. She looked tired and sick; her eyes were not as sparkling as Ah Pau's. She sat on the ground with a small chicken cage in front of her. There was only one hen inside. It squatted, with its head crooked to one side. Its eyes were ready to go to sleep. I hesitated for a few seconds, trying to figure out if I should tell her that I was Cripple Yip's schoolmate, but I didn't.

I continued to the cake stand. There were a few people waiting for the cakes that were being fried. I waited, too, but I looked toward Cripple Yip's grandma. A few people passed in front of her. She raised up her head to say, "Buy the big hen," but no one stopped.

After I got the cakes, I walked back past her. She was pleading to another lady to buy her big hen. When I gave the two cakes to Ah Pau, I said, "Ah Pau, look at that—"

"Don't just look. Eat, before a customer comes!"

I crammed the sizzling cake into my mouth, almost burning the roof of my mouth. Suddenly I had lost all interest in selling. I just kept my eyes on Cripple Yip's grandma. By that time, the crowd was even thinner than before I got the cakes. She was still raising her head while the people passed her space. Why didn't anyone stop? I wondered.

"What are you doing?" Ah Pau poked my ribs and reminded me, "Get the change."

"Oh, how much?" I suddenly realized that

the white-bearded old man had bought my last chicken fence.

"Give him back twenty cents change."

"Thank you," I said to the man.

After he left, Ah Pau questioned me. "What are you looking at? You're not concentrating on selling."

"Look at that old lady over there. No one even stops to look at her hen."

"Where?"

"See? The lady with the big bamboo hat, not far away from the cake cart."

She looked in the direction where I pointed. "Of course not, her hen looks half dead. Who would buy a dead hen, anyway?"

"But she's very disappointed. . . ."

"Why are you so interested in other people's business? Huh? Just keep your mind on your work instead of looking around."

"But she's Cripple Yip's grandma. . . ."

Ah Pau didn't hear me. She was busy with another customer. What did Cripple Yip's grandma feel when a lot of people stopped at the other stands, but none stopped at hers?

Would it make her feel a little better if someone just stopped for a few seconds? I wondered.

Ah Pau suddenly told me, "It's late. I'm going home to fix something to eat and see how Kee's doing. Are you tired?"

"Uh-uh."

"You can stay a little while if you want. Someone will come here late to get a good bargain."

I nodded.

She whispered in my ear, "You give all your money to me. I'm afraid you'll lose it."

"Uh-uh, it's my money. I'll take care of it."

"If no one buys the baby hats, you can bring them home and save them for the next farmers' market. You just stay as long as you want." She wanted to leave the stool for me, but I told her that I didn't want it.

"Are you sure you won't let me take your money home? It's a lot of money."

"No. It's my money. I want to take it home all by myself to show Kee."

"If you don't listen to me and lose it, you will regret it very much. Be careful when you give the change to the people."

"I will."

So she left. She took the stool and the bamboo pole with her.

Nobody asked me about the baby hats. I was tired, sleepy, and hungry. So I wrapped the last two baby hats inside the sheet to make a bundle. I didn't know why, but I walked slowly toward Cripple Yip's grandma. The hen had completely closed its eyes—it was still and looked dead.

"Buy the big hen," she said to me again. Her voice was weaker than before. I shook my head. Who would buy a dead hen, anyway? I wanted to say "I'm sorry" for not buying her dead hen and also for her loss of Cripple Yip. I had been wanting to say it so many times before. I didn't know why, but I couldn't say a word. I just passed her, and she watched me go. At that moment, I couldn't stand the way she looked. It reminded me of the sad look Cripple Yip had when she came back from seeing the principal. After I passed the carrot-cake cart and a couple of stalls, her sad look would not leave my mind. So I walked back to her and asked, "How much is it?" My voice was shaking.

"Oh, oh." She was surprised that I would return. She looked around and lowered her voice. "How much money do you have?"

"Eight *yuan* and eighty cents. I just sold all my chicken fences."

"Well . . ." She seemed to have difficulty speaking. I could barely hear her. "I will let you have it for eight *yuan* and eighty cents. I was supposed to sell it for nine *yuan*."

Without even thinking, I took all the money out of my pocket and gave it to her. She just said, "Thank you." Then she took the hen out of the cage and handed it to me. The hen's legs were stiff and cold, but the body was still a little warm.

"Thank you," she said. She looked straight into my eyes and smiled. "You are a very nice girl."

"Thank you," I said. I knew she was happy because someone had bought her hen, and I was happy, too, because I had done something that was much better than just saying "I'm sorry."

CHAPTER 17

"**I**'m home!" I called out loudly. Kee ran out to meet me. He seemed to have completely recovered from his diarrhea.

"Grandma said you did a good job! Where's the money?"

Oh, no! For the first time since I had bought the hen, I remembered that part of the money belonged to Kee and to Ah Pau, for the materials. "I . . ."

"Where's the money?" He stared at me and glanced at the dead hen, puzzled.

"I . . . I bought this hen with it."

"Are you crazy?"

I couldn't answer.

"The hen is dead! Are you crazy? Grandma!" Kee laughed in disbelief. "Ying bought a dead hen!"

Before I realized it, Ah Pau was standing in front of me with her eyes about to pop out. She was speechless for a while. "Who would be so stupid as to buy a dead hen? You're completely out of your mind! Was it from that old lady? Tell me! Tell me!" Ah Pau's gold-and-jade earrings swung violently, and her voice scared me.

"It's better than just saying 'I'm sorry,' Ah Pau," I cried. She had never before been that angry with me.

"You don't need to say anything!"

"You don't understand, Ah Pau."

"You are right. I *don't* understand. How

could an old lady cheat a ten-year-old girl like that? She should be ashamed of herself for the rest of her life!"

"She didn't cheat me. I asked her how much it was. She asked me how much I had, and I told her I had eight *yuan* and eighty cents. She said it was nine *yuan*, but she would sell it to me cheaper, for eight *yuan* and eighty cents."

"You used *all* the money for that? *Aiyah!* Eight *yuan* and eighty cents could buy two or three *live* chickens!"

All the time, Kee had been watching, like a spectator, laughing at my stupidity. But after he heard that I had spent all the money, including his, he jumped up, screaming. "You used *my* money, *too!*"

Ah Pau ordered me, "Go get the money back!"

"No, I don't want to."

Abruptly Kee snatched the hen from my arms. "No! No!" I tried to grab the hen back.

"You stupid!" Kee slapped me and almost

knocked me off my feet. Then he started running. Ah Pau called after him, giving him instructions. "The old lady is near the fried-carrot-cake cart. Hurry!"

Using one hand, I covered my face where Kee had slapped me, crying, "Please don't. Please don't." But it was no use. Kee had gone. I crossed my fingers and hoped that she had already left, and I was glad that Ah Pau didn't know that the lady was Cripple Yip's grandma. Otherwise, Kee could have gone to her house to get the money back, even if he couldn't find her at the farmers' market.

Finally, Kee came back. Breathless, he threw the hen at me and gave me a disgusted look. "Stupid! You pay the money back to me!"

Ah Pau stormed again, "Now you have to take the consequences. No lunch today! That will teach you a lesson, and don't expect me to give you the money for your camp-out!"

"I won't," I said quietly.

"What about me?" Kee stared at me as if he wanted to strangle me.

"And what about the money that we owe the store, huh? Did you think about that? You tell me!" Oh, I couldn't believe Ah Pau was talking to me like that. "You must not have thought about it! You don't know the value of money. You act as if you're a millionaire. Didn't you know that you worked for months just to get that little bit of money? Didn't you remember that you wouldn't even spend two cents for a fried carrot cake for yourself? How could you just waste all the money on an old lady you didn't even know!"

"She is—" I almost blurted out. "You don't understand, Ah Pau."

"Why don't I understand? I watched you being born. I have watched you grow. I know everything about you. You just didn't use your brain. Now, you tell me how you're going to pay back Kee and the store owner."

"I can pay Kee back when I get my *lai see* money next year."

Kee was writing and erasing on a piece of paper. When he heard Ah Pau mention his name, he exclaimed, "*Lai see* money again? I don't want to wait until next year! I want it now!"

There was no way I could pay back the money so quickly.

"And how about the store owner? I don't know how to face him," Ah Pau said.

I was silent. I stood with my head down, staring at the floor, but I did not regret what I had done.

"I have an idea. Take away her snack money to pay back the store owner," Kee suggested.

"That's a good idea," Ah Pau agreed.

Kee hurriedly wrote again. Then he held up the piece of paper and announced, "This is a treaty she has to sign."

I didn't know what a treaty was. Neither did Ah Pau.

Kee said, "In our history book, it says that after a war, a defeated country signs a treaty that is made up by the winning country. Now, she's the defeated country, and we're the victors. She has to agree with whatever the treaty says. She cannot reject any conditions. I'm going to read it:

1. I can't go to the camp for sure this year. I can't go next year until I completely pay back all the money I owe to Kee or other people. No debts before I can go.

2. To make up the money that I owe the store owner (total of four yuan and forty cents), I will not have snacks for 440 days.

3. I must pay back two yuan and twenty cents for Kee's chicken fences, plus interest, as soon as possible.

4. I can't have even one cent in my hand from now on while I am selling the chicken fences or other stuff. The money must be kept by Ah Pau or Kee until I pay back all the debts.

5. I can't have any lunch today.

"That's it. Now, sign it. No choice!"

Kee handed the paper to me. He thought that I would reject it, but I signed it at once, though I did not quite understand some of the points. I felt okay, although he said I was like a defeated country.

Kee signed his name next to mine and dated it: March 15, 1947.

"Grandma, you have to sign, too."

"Why? It's just a child's game," Ah Pau said.

"No, you have to, Grandma, so she can't deny it. At least you can be a witness so she can't weasel out of it later."

"Well . . ." Ah Pau hesitated, and I could tell she was a little embarrassed. "You know I don't know how to write my name."

"I can help you." Kee got his ink box, which held a piece of cotton soaked with ink. "Let me hold your thumb, Grandma."

So Kee held Ah Pau's right thumb and pressed it onto the black cotton, and then pressed it onto the paper. "That's what people do when they don't know how to read or write."

Kee was very happy after the treaty was signed. He and Ah Pau had their lunch while I stayed in my room. I heard Ah Pau say to Kee, "She doesn't regret it at all. I don't know what was in her mind."

CHAPTER 18

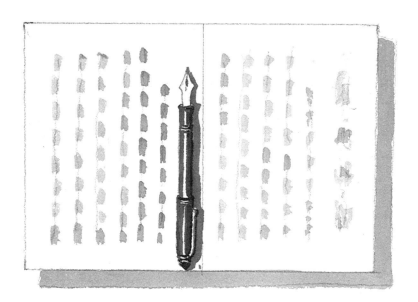

*T*he next day, on the way to school, something hit me in the back. It was a small rock. I turned to look and saw Ng Shing dash behind a mimosa tree. I ignored him and kept walking.

Another rock!

"You don't need to hide. I saw you already, Ng Shing," I called out. "If you keep bothering me, I'm going to tell on you!"

"Go ahead, Dead-Hen Buyer! Go ahead, Dead-Hen Buyer!" he sang all the way to school.

Many students stared at me. One girl I didn't know pointed to me and asked her friend, "Is that the one who bought a dead hen?"

Her friend nodded her head. Then they covered their mouths and giggled.

"Hey, Ying." Ming Ming and Ping Ping caught me from behind. Ping Ping asked, "Why did he call you Dead-Hen Buyer?"

Before I could answer her, three boys from my class—Lee On, Fong Sang, and Tan Sum—passed me and sang loudly, "Hey, Dead Hen! Stupid Dead-Hen Buyer!"

Ming Ming asked me, "Why are they all teasing you like that?"

"I bought a dead hen yesterday," I said.

"You did?"

They started to laugh out loud. It made my face feel hot. I walked away from them. I wanted to hide in the classroom, but the classroom was even worse. As I sat down at my desk, I saw that someone had written on the blackboard, "Who would buy a dead hen?" I didn't know who had written it, but I did know that it was about me.

Mrs. Yu had not come in yet, so I got up and erased it. Some boys teased me, saying, "Dead Hen! Dead Hen!" Ng Shing's devil voice was the loudest. Just as I returned to my seat, he went up and wrote it even bigger and higher on the board. I didn't want to erase it. Shing surely would just write it over again.

Ah Mei, who sat behind me now, asked, "Did you really buy a dead hen?"

"Yes."

She giggled and said, "Silly, why did you do that?"

"You don't understand," I said, turning my face back to the board sadly because even my best friend was laughing at me.

About that time, Mr. Hon came in. We were very surprised. "I am going to take Mrs. Yu's class for a while. She has to take some time off. Her mother is very ill."

I was thrilled, for I had had a crush on him since he had come to teach at our school last year. He was young, tall, and handsome. I had been wishing that I could be in the fifth grade soon so he could teach me literature. Yet it was my secret, and nobody knew except Kee, who had once sneaked a look at a paper on which I had written Mr. Hon's name many times. That was the reason Kee would tease me and say that I was love-sick whenever I was feeling low. Mr. Hon didn't know I had a crush on him; he didn't even know who I was.

"Yeung Ying's stomach is growling!" Shing announced loudly. My face flushed, not because I didn't have money to buy a snack, but because the whole class laughed. I hated him! I wished he would keep his mouth shut forever! It was so embarrassing, especially in front of Mr. Hon. Mr. Hon ignored Shing's comment, but said to Shing, "Raise your hand before you speak." Ng Shing was quiet.

Mr. Hon told us to take out our exercise books. He was going to give us some exercises

in class. As he was ready to write the assignment on the board, he noticed the words Ng Shing had written. If I had known that he would be in my class, I would have erased the words for sure. But it was too late now. I hoped he would understand why I bought the dead hen because he was special to me. But Mr. Hon laughed, asking, "Who would be stupid enough to buy a dead hen?"

"Yeung Ying did!" The whole class replied and laughed at the same time. I felt they were all pointing at me. I wished I were a magician and could turn myself into a bird and fly far away.

At once, Mr. Hon lost all the attraction he had held for me. He was not handsome anymore; now he was the same as the others.

"Is it true, Yeung Ying?"

My face felt hot again. I didn't know how to answer him.

"She's too ashamed to admit it," Shing answered.

"Shut up!" I yelled, and tears started rolling down my cheeks.

"Okay, stop all the teasing. And you," he said to Shing, "one more time without raising your hand to speak, and I will send you to the principal. Do you hear me?"

Ng Shing whispered, "Yes, sir." I could tell he was frightened for the first time since I had sat with him.

Two days later, Mr. Hon announced that we would each write something for the school composition contest, which was held every year. The prizes this year would be different. First prize would be two *yuan,* the total fee for the camping trip; second prize would be one *yuan* and twenty cents, and third prize would be one *yuan.* Everybody seemed thrilled, except me. I had never won a contest in my life.

Mr. Hon said that this year there was no particular topic and no word limit. He suggested, "You can write about anything you want. The best way is to write about something you are familiar with, or write about your feelings or your frustrations. It's much better than trying to write about something you haven't had any experience with." The whole class, including Shing, started writing, but I didn't have any idea what to write about. I wondered how the others had gotten inspiration so quickly.

For a long time my piece of paper was blank. I stared at the board, looked out the window, and glanced at the walls and the corners of the room, trying to think of something to write about, but I couldn't.

"You haven't started yet, Yeung Ying? There is only half a period left," Mr. Hon said, standing beside my desk.

"I don't know what to write about," I replied. I wished that the contest was voluntary.

"You can write about your feelings."

"What kind of feelings?"

"Well, like when you are sad, happy, or

frustrated. For example, you might write about why you bought the dead hen, and how you felt when people laughed at you."

"Do you think I should write about that?"

"Why not?"

"Okay, I'll try." I liked Mr. Hon again.

Then, without thinking about what Mrs. Yu had taught us about the three parts of the composition, I started writing.

I have been working very hard since New Year holiday to make chicken fences to get money for the camping trip. But I spent all my money to buy a dead hen. I spent Kee's and the store owner's, too. Therefore, Ah Pau was very mad, and Kee said that I was stupid. Everybody did, even my best friend. Kee also told me to sign a treaty that I didn't quite understand. But I signed it. The treaty said I couldn't go on the camping trip because I didn't have any money. I have to pay back the money to Kee and the store owner. So I won't have snack money for 440 days. Plus, I have to give every single cent to Kee until I have paid him. I didn't mind that treaty at all. I deserved it. But all my friends have treated me not very nice. I wish they could leave me alone, because they don't understand!

I bought the dead hen from Cripple Yip's grandmother. Why did I do that? Let me tell you. I had been wanting to say "I am sorry" to her after Cripple Yip died. But it was very difficult to say. I felt very bad for telling that Cripple Yip was coming out of the class when Ng Shing said I stole his money. If I knew she would drown, I would have never told the truth. I wish time could go back to that day so I could start all over. But my wish will never come true. At the farmers' market, I had another chance to tell her grandma I'm sorry, but I did not. There was no one who stopped to look at her hen. I couldn't stand the way she looked. It was very sad, and it reminded me of Cripple Yip. Therefore, I went back to buy the hen, even though I knew that the hen was already dead. I hoped she would feel a little bit better for someone buying her hen. I felt very good after that. I think that's much better than just saying, "I am sorry."

I don't regret that I can't go camping. But I am very upset about my schoolmates. Ng Shing threw rocks at me. He called me "Dead-Hen Buyer" all the way to school and back home. Now, some boys in school call me "Stupid Dead-Hen Buyer" or "Dead Hen." And girls I don't know pointed at me and said, "That's the girl," and the girls I know still ask me why I did that. They think I was crazy. Yet I didn't complain to Ah Pau or Kee. They might say that I deserved it. I wish all of them would just leave me alone. That's all.

I wrote it all down very fast without even stopping a second to think. I looked at the others, especially Ah Mei. She looked very nervous. She always wanted to be the best, and she usually was. She had not even started to copy hers over. I didn't want to go back to reread or copy it over.

The bell rang. I was the first one to turn in my paper. Mr. Hon gave the class ten more minutes. But Ah Mei was still not ready to turn hers in. She was the last to finish.

CHAPTER 19

*I*t was warm. Mimosa trees along the road to our school were blossoming with tiny red flower buds all over. The vegetable gardens at both sides of the school entrance had tender greens growing row after row. Birds were calling each other, jumping from tree to tree at our school. It was a beautiful spring day. There were only three days before the camping trip. Mr. Hon was going to announce the contest winners. The whole class was quiet.

"Wong Tai, a sixth-grader, won first prize. Wong Cheung, also a sixth-grader, won second prize. And the third-prize winner is in this class," Mr. Hon said mysteriously.

All of us looked in Ah Mei's direction. Her face flushed.

"The student who won third prize is—"

"Chan Mei," all of us said.

"Uh-uh." Mr. Hon shook his head.

Ah Mei's forehead broke out in a sweat while all of us mumbled about who it could be.

"Quiet, class. "It's—" Mr. Hon looked in my direction. "Yeung Ying!"

"Me!" I exclaimed, not believing my ears. I felt the whole class staring at me. I turned to Ah Mei and asked, "Did Mr. Hon say it was me?"

"Yes," Ah Mei's face was pale. Her voice was not very happy. "I never would have thought that it was you."

"I wouldn't, either."

"Please stand up, Yeung Ying," Mr. Hon said to me. I stood up. I felt like a celebrity all of a sudden. I felt as if I were floating up in the sky in a dream—up . . . up . . . up. . . . Then I was awakened suddenly by the clapping of the whole class.

Mr. Hon told the class to be quiet again. He said to me, "Congratulations, Yeung Ying. You copy it neatly at home. We're going to put your paper on the school bulletin board."

I went up to get the paper. I was still feeling as if I were walking on clouds. Mr. Hon was wearing a white, Western-style, long-sleeve shirt and navy blue pants. He looked very handsome. When I got my paper, he suddenly lowered his voice and whispered, "I apologize."

I looked at him. I didn't know what he was talking about.

"I apologize for the day I laughed when I read what was on the board. It just slipped out. I wasn't thinking. I am sorry." He thrust out

his hand, and I didn't know what to do. Finally, he took my hand and shook it. I had never shaken hands with a man, especially a man I had a crush on!

After I got the paper from Mr. Hon, he told me to read it out loud to the class. Never before had any teacher told me to do that.

"Me?"

"Yes, you," he said. "I want the class to understand something."

I didn't understand what he meant. I stood in front of his desk and read my composition. My hands were trembling, my face was hot, and my voice was shaking. But the class was quiet. I felt very awkward reading my own composition. After I finished reading it, Mr. Hon told me to return to my seat. I still felt as if I were in a dream. Mr. Hon then asked, "Class, what do you think? What do we owe Yeung Ying?"

They looked at each other. They were not sure what they owed me. They started to mumble. Mr. Hon gave them a hint. "Think about it, class. Why did Yeung Ying buy a dead hen from Yip On's grandma? What was your attitude toward her? And what are you going to do?"

The whole class was silent again. After a few minutes, Ah Mei raised her hand. "Apologize."

"Yes, that is right. I hope you all sincerely apologize to Yeung Ying during recess."

They did. Some of them apologized in person. Some of them handed me notes to ask for forgiveness. Even Shing mumbled, without looking at me, "Sorry," and quickly retreated.

While I was running home from school, I had a brainstorm—since the school was going to pay me one *yuan* for the camping fee, I might have a chance to go this year, if Ah Pau would lend me one *yuan*. I ran home at full speed.

Kee was waiting for me at the front door with his bookbag still in his hand. He asked me anxiously, "How could *you* win it? Let me see your paper."

"No! I want to show Ah Pau first!"

Ah Pau came out of the house. "I won, Ah Pau!" I called out.

"I know. Kee has already told me. I want you to read your composition to me. I want to know what you were writing about."

"Let *me* read it." Kee tried to grab my paper.

"No! I can read it myself. I had to read it in my class, and I'm going to copy it. They're going to put it on the school bulletin board."

"Really?" they both asked.

"Really! And everybody apologized to me, even Ng Shing! And Mr. Hon shook my hand."

"Oh, I can't believe it. What did they apologize for?" Ah Pau asked.

"You'll see. Let me read it to you. The title is"—I thought for a few seconds and said, "'Who Would Buy a Dead Hen?'"

Ah Pau's mouth dropped wide open. Kee looked over my shoulder at the paper while I read the composition. After I finished reading it, Kee grabbed my paper and read it again. Then he gave it back to me without any comment. Ah Pau wept, saying, "I didn't know that you had such a tender heart. I thought I understood you, but I really didn't."

I jumped at the chance at once. "Ah Pau, may I go to the camp-out now? See, the school will pay one *yuan* for me, and if you lend me one *yuan*, I'll have enough."

"Well, I wish I could, Ying. I didn't tell you. I went to the store to ask the owner if we could pay him back the cost of materials later. But his business wasn't doing well, and he had to ask me to pay him back and let you pay me back little by little. And I thought he was fair for letting us take his materials months ahead. So I scraped together every cent I had to pay him. I'm sorry. I wish I could afford your trip."

"That's okay, Ah Pau. I can wait until next year. I had planned for next year, anyway."

That day, a little before supper, Kee took out the treaty from a drawer and canceled points 1, 3, and 4.

"What are you doing, Kee?" Ah Pau asked.

"I canceled most of the treaty. I don't need her to pay back the chicken fence money."

"Make sure you cancel the one about the snack fee," Ah Pau suggested.

"No, leave it there," I told her.

"Why?"

"That money is supposed to be the store owner's, not mine."

"But I have already paid him."

"It's unfair to you, Ah Pau."

"You'll be hungry, though."

"Just let her pay for it, Grandma. That's her decision."

"But she'll be hungry at school," Ah Pau mumbled.

"She could fix cold rice to eat before she goes to school."

"Oh, yes. I could fix you some rice with hot tea in it. Are you hungry now?"

"Yes. But I don't want to eat now. I have to finish copying my composition first."

"Hey, don't expect me to cancel another treaty later on. I want you to get that idea right out of your mind!"

I laughed, but I didn't say anything.

CHAPTER 20

O ne day before the camp-out, all the teachers read my composition on the bulletin board. They were touched by my behavior, and together they donated one *yuan* and thirty cents to me for the camp-out. I didn't need to wait until next year!

On the camp-out, when I had to stand

guard at night all by myself, I was so scared that I sneaked back inside the tent. I heard noises outside and thought it was ghosts. But the next morning, all our cooking equipment was gone! The students from another school had sneaked in and taken our wok and pans. Our group lost the game. Because of that, I acquired another name—Chicken. But it was still fun.

There is even more. One morning about two months after I bought the dead hen, Mr. Leung, the school secretary, sent a note to my class, saying the principal wanted to see me. I was nervous, and the whole class sweated for me. I dragged myself to the office. I could hear my heart beating.

"Someone wants to see you," the principal told me simply. I was too frightened to ask him who wanted to see me.

"Follow me," he said.

So I followed him into a guest room. A man about my uncle's age stood up when I came in. He looked like a city person.

"This is Yeung Ying," the principal said to the stranger.

The stranger bowed to the principal, saying, "Thank you. Thank you, sir."

"You are welcome," the principal replied and retreated.

Now there was nobody in the guest room but us. I wondered why the stranger wanted to see me.

"So you're Yeung Ying," the stranger said, motioning me to sit down beside him. He looked kind. "I have been looking for you for quite a while."

What did he mean? I was very anxious to know.

"Do you remember the old lady you bought the hen from at the farmers' market?"

"Yes, sir," I answered timidly.

"I am her third cousin, from Canton. She sent this to you along with a letter. She couldn't write, so I wrote it for her." He handed me a package.

I took the package. It was wrapped with a big, faded black handkerchief. "What is it?"

"You can open it and see, but be careful, extremely careful."

He helped me to untie the handkerchief. Inside was a transparent green vase. It was about three inches tall, and carved on it were a dragon and a phoenix.

Suddenly he whispered to me, "This is an antique jade vase—her family heirloom, passed from generation to generation."

What was I going to do with this antique? I thought. I was disappointed. I couldn't wear it, I couldn't play with it, I couldn't buy something with it. I would rather have a doll or a bead necklace than a vase. But I didn't say anything to him. I didn't understand why Cripple Yip's grandma would send me that.

The stranger seemed to understand what I was thinking, and suggested, "You read the letter. It will explain everything."

So I read the letter. It said:

To the little girl who bought my dead hen:
How awful I felt and how ashamed of myself—

cheating a little innocent girl who is about the same age as my only granddaughter. I have been feeling guilty ever since I sold the hen to you. I have been wanting to ask you to forgive me, but my health wouldn't allow me to do so—I have been lying in bed ever since. And I was afraid that I wouldn't have a chance to apologize to you in person. Will you accept my apology? I hope you will. Otherwise, I will not be able to rest in peace when I am gone.

To try to make up what I owe you, I am giving you my family heirloom, which is the only valuable thing in my house. I didn't want to sell it, even when I was in the most critical condition, for that is the only family treasure I have. I have valued it very much. Now, I give it to you to keep, to make up what I owe you.

How I wish I could find you, see you in person to give this to you—you reminded me so much of my only granddaughter, who left me.

There was a fingerprint at the end of the letter, like Ah Pau's on the treaty. I wanted to tell her that I had never regretted buying the dead hen from her. I said, "She doesn't need to give her family treasure to me. I will return it to her."

The stranger gently touched my hand. "It's very kind of you, but she is already gone."

"What?"

"About one month ago. I promised that I would give this to you in person. I think she will rest in peace now. All you need to do is treasure it as she treasured it."

"I will," I promised him. Suddenly I felt that even if someone offered me a thousand bead necklaces, I would never let it go. "Thank you," I told the stranger. "Thank you for all your trouble to find me."

I carefully brought the antique jade vase home. "Ah Pau! Ah Pau!" I called out loudly.

Ah Pau rushed out from the kitchen. Her gold-and-jade earrings swung wildly. She asked, "What's the matter?"

"Look! Look at this!"

Ah Pau let out a sigh and said, "You scared

me! I thought something had happened to you."

"It did!" I carefully untied the big handkerchief on the dining table. "Look!"

Kee walked in from school.

"Where did you find it?" they asked. Both of them thought that it was something I had found for my junk collection.

"Guess!"

"Just tell me," Kee said, picking up the vase to examine it.

"Be careful. It's an antique," I told him.

"Antique?" Kee looked closely at the vase. Then he walked toward the courtyard where the light was brighter to check it. He said, "I can't tell."

"Let me see," Ah Pau said. Kee handed it to Ah Pau. Ah Pau also raised it up in the air to examine it. She said, "I don't know about antiques, but the jade alone would cost a fortune! See, the whole piece of jade is transparent, so green and so clear. Look at the handwork! Where did you find such a nice vase?"

"Can't you guess?" I smiled and said, "Do

you remember the old lady I bought the dead hen from? She felt sorry for cheating me, so she gave it to me."

"She did! Well, I misjudged her. But you shouldn't accept such an expensive gift. I want you to return it to her."

"But she's gone."

"What?" Ah Pau almost dropped the vase on the ground.

"She died a month ago. That's why she wanted me to keep it for her."

Ah Pau stared at me. Her eyes looked frightened and her face seemed suddenly pale.

"What's wrong, Ah Pau?"

"Hurry . . . throw that thing away."

"Why?" both Kee and I asked at the same time.

"Just do what I say. Throw it away! Throw it into the pond so no one can find it!"

I took the vase back from her and said, "No. I want to keep it."

"Do you know you should never take anything that belonged to a dead person who was a stranger to you?"

I had heard that before. If you did, the spirit of the owner would haunt you no matter where you went.

"But she knew who I was."

"Did she know your name? Did she?"

Ah Pau's voice frightened me. I was about to cry. I said, "No. But . . . but she asked her cousin to find me and she also wrote a letter to me." I took the letter from my bookbag. Kee grabbed it.

When Ah Pau noticed that I was about to cry, she embraced me, and her voice was softer than before. She said, "I know it's very hard for you. But for your own sake, just throw it into the pond and forget it. Ah Pau has never guided you wrong."

So I cried all the way to the pond. I cried for the loss of the vase. I cried for breaking my promise to the man. I cried for the old lady's disappointment at my not treasuring her family heirloom. But most of all, I cried because I was scared.

As I was looking for a good spot in the

pond to throw the vase, Kee ran, breathless, to the granite rock shore. Before he reached me, he called, "Have you thrown it away yet?"

"No. I was getting ready to."

"Don't!"

"Ah Pau will let me keep it?" I asked.

"She didn't say so. But we have to go. She's waiting for us."

"Go where?"

"Go to where Cripple Yip lived before."

"Why?"

"I don't know. Grandma said she had second thoughts after I read the letter to her. She was afraid it would irritate the old lady's spirit if you don't do what she asked. So let's go, hurry!"

We ran back to the village. Ah Pau was waiting for us in front of our house with a basket full of worship materials.

We stopped at the dirt road in front of the old lady's hut, the same place where Ah Mei and I had lingered before. The door was closed, and the chickens were gone. The vegetable patch had disappeared, and weeds grew high everywhere.

Ah Pau faced the hut and respectfully placed all the worship materials and the vase on the edge of the road. Several children with ragged clothes came over to watch.

Ah Pau started to burn the paper worship material and chanted prayers. Then she said to us, "Kneel down and kowtow three times." We knelt down and bowed our heads to the ground, and Ah Pau did the same.

Before Ah Pau lit the firecrackers she had brought, she instructed us, "Say, 'Please go somewhere else.'"

Kee and I looked at each other, not quite understanding, but we mumbled, "Please go somewhere else."

The children giggled.

When the firecrackers exploded, the air smelled like gunpowder. Ah Pau put the vase into the basket. Before we left, she said again, much louder this time, "Ying will take care of the vase. Go somewhere else!"

At home, Ah Pau wrapped the jade vase with a bright red piece of material. Then she put it in a tin to protect it.

After she had removed a clay tile from the kitchen floor near the stove where we stacked pine straw, Ah Pau said, "Now, you put it in yourself."

I lay down on my stomach and placed the tin into the hole beneath the floor, beside my family's other valuable things. Then Ah Pau put the tile back and replaced the pine straw on top of it. She smiled and declared, "That's what is meant by saying, 'The hay covers the pearl!'"

"Thank you, Ah Pau!" I said, hugging her. "I'm not scared anymore."

GLOSSARY

bok choi — A green, leafy Chinese vegetable used in stir-frying or to make soup.

catty — A unit of measurement equal to approximately one and one-third pounds.

gwa gee — Melon seeds dyed red that are eaten at Chinese New Year.

hell money — Paper money for the worship of spirits.

jeen dui — A round, deep-fried pastry with sweet puffed rice inside eaten at Chinese New Year.

ju sax — A red powderlike mineral used as a sedative in Chinese medicine.

jung — Salty or sweet, sticky rice wrapped in a banana or lily leaf.

Kung hay fat choi — A phrase used at Chinese New Year to wish people wealth and prosperity in the new year.

lai see money — Money given at Chinese New Year to the younger generation by married relatives and friends. It is given in a red paper pocket.

leen go — Chinese pound cake eaten during Chinese New Year.

phoenix — A mythical bird that lives for several hundred years and is burned up in fire, then rises from the ashes to start another long life; the symbol of immortality.

Po Chai pills — Chinese medicine for diarrhea.

teet da jow — Chinese liniment for bruises and sprains.

tong cheong sam — Traditional Chinese tunic.

yau gok — Sweet, deep-fried, crescent-shaped pastry eaten at Chinese New Year.

yuan — Chinese unit of money. One hundred cents equals one *yuan*.